sinnamon & golds

LADY MARIE

Cover design by Aubree Pynn

Editing by A.K. Edits

Formatting by Author Mya

contents

Content Warning   vii

1. Sinna   1
2. Sinna   11
3. Gideon   23
4. Sinna   27
5. Gideon   33
6. Sinna   39
7. Gideon   43
8. Gideon   49
9. Sinna   55
10. Sinna   65
11. Gideon   69
12. Gideon   81
13. Sinna   87
14. Sinna   95
15. Gideon   99
16. Gideon   105
Want more of your favorite messy duo?   111
A Final Word   113

Acknowledgments   115
Also by Lady Marie   117

For Kai, who not only pushes me to be better, but makes me cackle while she does it.
No other editor could ever compare.

And for anyone who ever wanted to get their lick back. You deserve.

content warning

This book features explicit sexual content and brief on-page violence. This one is messy y'all, but it's all in good fun.

.

CHAPTER ONE

sinna

MAMA HAZEL:

Alright now, it's that time of year again.
Y'all already know why I'm here and what
to do. Let's talk Thanksgiving logistics
because ain't nobody showing up to my
house empty-handed. Everybody better
click the link and sign up for something
or you'll be spending the holiday by your
damn self.

THE SOUND THAT ESCAPED ME WAS SOMETHING OF A MIX
between a groan and a cackle. How and why was I still in
this thread? Checking the timestamp, it looked like the
message had been sitting in my inbox for ten minutes, just
long enough for me to grab myself a snack after shutting
down my work computer. Submitting my lesson plans had
taken all of my energy, so the only thing on my mind right
now was curling up on the couch with my favorite blanket.
No distractions. Before I had the chance to delete the
thread, another message came through.

MAMA HAZEL:

And Rose, don't you even think about bringing another nasty ass experimental pie like the one you tried to give us at Vera's house last year. If I even think you're about to try some mess, I swear I'll drive the ninety minutes it takes to get to your house and pop you right in your already fat lip.

Now that message got a full-blown cackle out of me. Ms. Hazel was a certified hot ass mess, but I knew her message threatening her younger sister was dead serious. I'd actually pay money to see the older woman make good on her promise. The memory of the avocado, pine nut, and key lime pie Rose made last Thanksgiving was still engraved in my mind. That damn thing left all six people brave enough to try it sick and throwing up for hours and all three bathrooms in the house occupied. It did not make for a pretty picture. Last I heard, their other sister Vera still couldn't look her neighbors in the eye after the mess she made when she had to use their bathroom instead. No one wanted to take a chance on going for a two-peat.

AUNT ROSE:

But I have a really good sweet potato pie recipe this time around!

Oh, hell no. There were only two sweet potato pies I indulged in: mine and Queen Patti's herself. Even if that wasn't the case, I sure as hell wouldn't be tasting one made by Rose. Thank goodness I wouldn't have to worry about it this year.

MAMA HAZEL:

No. Absolutely not. I already signed you up to bring two cases of water.

MAMA HAZEL:

Besides, you know sweet potato pie is already spoken for.

And now it was officially time for me to exit the conversation since it was clear where this was headed. I set the phone down, vowing to remove myself from the message thread—*again*—when it wasn't so fresh and no one was paying attention. For now, muting it would just have to do the trick. Just because everyone in the group chat was about to spend the next hour discussing how I couldn't possibly be bringing the pies in question since Vontae and I had been broken up for five months and therefore I would not be attending the festivities didn't mean I had to subject myself to the conversation.

"What they do this year is not your business," I whispered to myself as I got comfortable on my sectional and grabbed the remote.

For the last two years, me joining Von's family for holidays and other special occasions hadn't even been a question. I'd claimed family status at every one of those gatherings because that was exactly how they'd always treated me—like family. From the moment Von first introduced me to his mama, she literally pulled me into her bosom and called me her daughter. It seemed to take only a matter of weeks before I was closer to her than I'd ever been with my own parents. Don't get me wrong, I love my family, but with them being all the way in Austin, Texas and me being in Acacia Hills, Virginia, traveling back and forth just wasn't something I did often. I'd made it a point to get out of Texas as soon as the opportunity arose and my daddy...well, he'd never really gotten over it. Despite my being twenty-seven years old, he still thought he had a say in how I lived my life. Being able to bond with Von's family just made the distance and decision to make my visits home few and far in between that much easier.

This year, though, it looked like I'd have to figure out different plans because as much as I loved her, Ms. Hazel's family was not an option.

***

Ignoring Mama Hazel so many times caused me literal pain.

The first day wasn't so bad. It actually didn't faze me at all. Day two, she called twice, first while I was running errands and the second time just as I was settling in to watch an episode of my favorite Real Housewives franchise. Now here we were, three days and two more calls in. I could give credit where credit was due. She hadn't called me immediately after sending the message in the group chat, which was what I'd initially expected. A week later, though, apparently Ms. Hazel's goal was to wear me down. Kudos to her because, well, it worked.

With a deep breath that barely did the job of calming my nerves, I answered the phone with a simple, "Hey, mama."

"Oh, so your phone does work? Chile, I was starting to worry you'd lost your job and they'd cut you off. You know, since my calls and messages kept going unanswered."

I wanted to snicker so bad but managed to control myself. If there was one thing Ms. Hazel was going to do, it was throw shade at any and everybody. I couldn't say I didn't see it coming.

"No, nothing cut off over here. I've just been really busy with work. You know how classrooms get around the holidays."

"Mhmm. They surely must have you running around like you're missing your head. You've been duckin' and dodgin' me like I'm a damn bill collector. About to have my feelings hurt out here."

This time I did actually giggle. "Still dramatic, I see."

"The only way I know how to be." She laughed along with me. "Besides, it's been weeks since we last talked. Before Halloween, if I'm not mistaken."

She was right. We spoke a lot more often than my own mom and I did. I knew for a fact I called her more often than her damn son. Our bond was something serious. Going more than a week without reaching out just wasn't a thing for us. The last few months, though, I'd felt the need to put some distance between us. It wasn't because I'd stopped loving her—I don't think there was anything that could've made that happen. But the longer Von and I went without getting back together, the more she felt the need to bring him up to me. The more she brought him up, the more irritated it made me, so I'd started putting up a few walls and spacing out calls. Having her call me out on it, though? I couldn't help but feel bad about it.

"I know, and I'm sorry, mama."

"It's okay, baby. I just miss my partner in crime, is all. Housewife Sunday just isn't the same without you."

"And it definitely isn't the same without you. I can only imagine how much hollering you were doing last week during that trip to Spain."

Her laugh matched my own. "Chiiiile, don't even get me started. Just promise me you won't make me watch the next episode without you."

"Promise."

"Good. Now in the meantime, I have another way you can make it up to me. Whip up a few of your sweet potato pies for Thanksgiving dinner on Thursday."

Shit. Guess I walked right into that one. For a second, my mind actually allowed me to forget exactly why she was calling me in the first place.

"*Drop off* some sweet potato pies? Sure. Actually, if I can get to the store tomorrow, I could probably bring them by Wednesday mor—"

"Now what sense does it make for you to bring them to me on Wednesday if you're going to be here on Thursday?"

Of course she wasn't going to make this easy. Closing my eyes, I took another deep breath. "Mama—"

"Oh no, don't *mama* me. Baby, you have to come. It's tradition."

A laugh bubbled out of me, even if I didn't want it to. "Please. I don't think something that's only been happening for a couple years can really count as an actual tradition."

"It does if I say it does," she shot back matter-of-factly. Before I had the chance to say anything else, she added, "Have you already made other plans? Because if you've decided to go see your parents this year, baby, I think that's a great idea."

That idea may have crossed my mind, but I'd realized two weeks ago spending an extended weekend listening to my father chastise me for my life choices while my mother played happy homemaker in the cabin they rented in Colorado with both sets of grandparents and whoever else decided to come along was a lot more than I could bear.

My hesitation must've given her the answer she was looking for. "That'll be a no, then? And we both know none of your lil' friends or coworkers get down in the kitchen like I do. So instead of spending Thanksgiving by yourself, come spend it with people who love you."

When she put it that way, the option didn't sound half-bad. My current plans had me spending the day by myself, getting an early start on decorating my apartment for Christmas, and watching some of my favorite holiday movies. Going to her house would certainly save me the trouble of having to cook for myself. There were always more than enough leftovers for anyone who wanted them to take home. Still, as much as I might love her, being in her home with my ex was not my vision of a holiday well spent. No, relishing in my own company was a much better choice.

"You know I appreciate the offer, but I'll be fine."

"Give me one good reason you won't come."

"Vontae Brooks," I said simply. Ms. Hazel meant well, but her pushing was going to send me over the edge if it went on much longer, so giving her the truth was the only way to make her let this entire thing go. At least, I thought it was.

"First off, you cannot keep letting that knucklehead

child of mine run you off from having a good time. Just because he decided to lose the good sense the Lord gave him and let you go means I have to suffer? Doesn't seem fair to me," she scoffed.

"Aren't you the one always talking about how life isn't fair?"

"Nope, you must have me confused with someone else."

Rolling my eyes, I stood up from the counter and made my way into my living room, cup of warm cider in hand. If I ever got out of this conversation, I was going to take a much-deserved nap.

"Second, Von won't be an issue because he won't be there."

"What?" I choked out. Taking a sip of my drink as she made that little revelation almost had my life flashing before my eyes. Vontae missing a holiday with his mama? His favorite holiday at that? Sounded like bullshit to me. "Since when does your son miss Thanksgiving or any family function you're hosting?"

"Since his job decided he needs to work through the holiday if he has any hope of getting into their managers' training program. Trust me, I threw a fit and gave him an earful. But he's already screwed up his personal life. No need for him to mess up his professional one, too. He'll just have to make do with the plate or two I'll put aside for him, which means you officially have no reason not to come."

An understanding but weak smile spread across my face. Just by her tone, I could tell she was going to have a hard time with Von missing dinner. Ever since her husband passed away a few years ago, she'd been holding on to Vontae for dear life. Even though he would most likely be over there on Friday and she'd have a house full of guests to keep her occupied, not having her baby boy seated at the table would be different from what she was used to. One thing about Ms. Hazel Brooks, she did not handle different very well. Couple that with me not being there either and well, it suddenly made complete sense why she was pressing the issue.

Still…

"How about I come over Sunday morning so we can do brunch, and you can show me all the stuff you didn't need but purchased anyway on Black Friday? And you can fill me in on all the drama I missed at dinner." That was the best I had to offer her at the moment.

Neither one of us said anything for a while, letting silence fill the line. Finally, she relented. "Okay. If you're sure you don't want to come, I won't force you. No matter how much I really want to."

"Thank you. It's very much appreciated, mama."

"Mhmm, I suppose."

"I can still bring the pies over, though. Anything to keep Aunt Rose from trying her hand at it."

She groaned into the receiver as if the mere thought was painful. Hell, it probably was. "No, it's okay, baby. A couple Patti pies should do the trick, though they won't be quite the same as having your recipe."

"Well, I'll make you one anyway and just bring it with me on Sunday."

"Mkay, baby." With a heavy sigh that was surely done for dramatic effect, she said, "Well, let me get on off this phone. This house and these greens are not going to clean themselves."

"Okay, mama. Love you." Despite me turning down her offer, I truly did love her like she was my own mother.

"I know, baby. Love you too."

sinna

"AND SEE, THIS IS WHY I TOLD YOUR ASS TO JUST COME ON vacation with me."

"Catiya, right now is not the time for an I-told-you-so moment," I said, rolling my eyes even though I knew she couldn't see me. My hand ran over my freshly bleached and close-cut head. The way my barber lined me up and made sure I looked good was the highlight of my day at this point.

"Actually, it's the perfect time. Here I am lounging next to the pool in Miami with only twenty-four hours to go before my weeklong cruise, and meanwhile, you're going to be looking sad and pitiful with a Hungry Man TV dinner all by yourself, playing hide and go seek with your ex's mother on arguably one of the most annoying holidays of the year." She kissed her teeth. "And don't even think about rolling your eyes again 'cause I know you already did it once."

I snickered because yes, my best friend since college freshman orientation clearly knew me too well. She was right, though. I should've taken her up on her offer to crash her vacation, but at the time, I'd thought I could stomach spending Thanksgiving with my family. I might have blamed the very overpriced plane ticket and horrible ass weather predictions when I broke the news to my mom, but we both knew better.

Catiya was only giving me shit now because I'd spent the last twenty minutes telling her about my phone call with Ms. Hazel. She'd been very supportive of my mission to stay at home and preserve my peace until this latest development. She was rude as hell for the Hungry Man dinner comment, though, especially since the two grocery stores and one Amish market I'd managed to get to today weren't making my task of putting together a dinner for one easy. I was still at the latter, and it seemed like everyone and their mama was in here. Why did I insist on procrastinating on every little thing?

"Just so we're clear, you don't know everything, miss ma'am." Checking my ticket, it looked like they were seven people away from calling my number at the produce stall.

"There you go, lying through your pretty ass teeth. What have I told you about that?" cackled Catiya.

Before I could respond, a flash of gold caught my eyes. "Speaking of pretty ass teeth," I mumbled.

The sound of my bestie asking, "Whose pretty teeth?" barely registered as I took in the finest piece of chocolate I'd seen in quite a long time standing just a few feet in front of me. His short locs were pulled away from his face and situated on top of his head, granting me license to watch as his dark eyes scanned the stall for something in particular. He wore a gold chain with a jeweled cross around his neck, but that wasn't what caught my attention. He'd been laughing, probably courtesy of whatever or whoever was on the other end of the earbud he was wearing, putting the gold grill covering his bottom row of teeth on display. The mustache and goatee that framed his plump lips only added to the package.

I fidgeted, thighs clenching as my pussy thumped when he turned and smiled in my direction, giving me an even better view. When did fine ass men like this start coming to the market? Was this what the world had to offer when you didn't rely mostly on takeout and grocery delivery services?

"Bitch, are you listening to me?" a voice screeched in my ear, snapping me out of whatever trance this man had put me in.

"Yes, bitch, damn!" I was lying through my damn teeth, and we both knew it.

"Well, I can't tell! I've called your name no less than four times. What the hell has you acting so spacey? Ain't no damn vegetables that interesting."

"Girl, please. You distracted me so much with all your fussing, I had to make sure they didn't call my number yet."

My eyes never left their gold-adorned target, not even when he turned away from me. That was fine. He had plenty on display to offer me from the back with the way he was filling out his letterman jacket and those sweatpants. I loved a nigga with a grill, and this one? This one looked like he talked big shit and carried a big dick to match.

"Yeah, whatever. Listen, I'm finna go back to my room and get in a nap before I decide on dinner. Call me when you're ready to start telling the truth since all you seem to want to do today is lie to me."

I barely registered the call ending because Golds himself was walking toward me. His gait, even in those few steps, let me know I was right about what he was carrying between his legs. Once he was in front of me, it was clear he stood somewhere around five foot eleven to my five foot nine. Between my height and two-hundred thirty-five pound weight mark, I'd been told more than a few times my frame could be intimidating. This man right here, though, didn't seem the least bit fazed.

"How you doing, thick mama?"

The deep bass of his voice set off every nerve ending I had. How dare this nigga have the audacity to sound like that on top of the way he looked? He was quickly checking off boxes on my 'top five reasons to lay it low and spread it wide' list without even trying. And considering how long it'd been since I'd actually done the very thing my list was made for, that wasn't an easy feat.

"Thick mama? That's how you talk to strangers?" I asked, scrunching up my nose, attempting to be irritated. If the name had come from anyone who didn't look like him then I wouldn't have to try hard. The way he smiled at me though, showing off his pearly whites and striking golds, made me think maybe he was saying just what I wanted to hear.

He chuckled. "It is when they look as good as you do. And when they stare just as hard as you've been for the last few minutes. One bold act deserves another, right?"

My lips tipped up in a small smirk. "Okay, you might've ate that a lil' bit." *But shit, I'd rather have you eating me.* "So, one bold stranger to another, how can I help you?"

"What's your number, if you don't mind me asking?"

"Damn, so you just not about to waste any time, huh?"

This time he gave me a full-bodied laugh, the sound wrapping around me like the warmest hug. "Nah, I meant your number for the produce stall." He gestured behind himself, and my eyes followed his hand toward the number on the screen.

"Oh," I said, a little more embarrassed than I expected to be. Maybe I needed to pump my brakes on the flirting a bit if he wasn't on that type of time. "Seventy-eight." According to the number on the screen, there were now only two people in front of me.

"Six," he said, holding up his own ticket. Damn, I hadn't even realized enough people had come through in search of a ticket that the dispenser had started a fresh set of numbers. "It's been a minute since I've been out here. Just trying to figure out how long this wait time is about to be 'cause truth be told, a nigga got other shit to do. This wasn't even on my agenda for the day for real."

"Got stuck doing the last-minute shop for mom?" I teased.

"Mom and auntie. And I left the list at home."

"Well, you better have a perfect memory. You know the elders do not play when it comes to family meals."

He laughed again, giving me the sudden urge to swoon. Was that something people actually did? Shit, maybe it was time to find out.

"Don't worry, I've got it handled."

"Sure you do," I said with a laugh of my own. "Unfortunately, I don't think I'll be any help on the wait time assessment since the market isn't usually on my agenda either. If it was, maybe I would've known better than to come two days before Thanksgiving."

"Damn. Guess we both drew the short straw." Sliding his hand down his face, he asked, "You been here a while?"

I checked my phone for the time. "Maybe like twenty-five minutes? Seems like most people are just grabbing a couple things and getting out of here. They don't really have much left, which makes this even more irritating."

His head dipped in a quick nod of understanding.

Another minute or two passed, the sounds of the market and shoppers floating around us while we both busied ourselves with our phones before he decided to break the silence.

"Listen." He brought one hand up to massage his jawline. He had to know the shit was distracting, and if he didn't, I would gladly be the first to tell him. "Like I said before, there's someplace else I gotta be, so I really ain't got time to be waiting around here while they make their way through another thirty people. So, that being said, you tryna do a nigga a favor?"

"There you go, being bold again. How exactly are you gonna assume you're entitled to a favor when I don't really know you? Especially if that favor is switching tickets. It's automatically a no."

"You got a real slick mouth, I see." His tongue darted out across his lips, and I felt a thump between my thighs again. "But it's not even like that, ma. The only thing I'm proposing is for you to let me grab the few lil' items I need when you go up there to get your stuff. Not trying to take your place or anything. Just looking for a little assistance."

He came in a half-step closer. "And as far as you not knowing me, we could easily change that. If you're interested." His eyes scanned me, and I felt the caress of it from the top of my blonde head to the bottom of my white toes.

Another number was called, leaving one person standing between me and freedom.

"So, I hear how this will help you out," I started, shaking off the effects of his gaze, "but you haven't really said how helping you would be beneficial for me."

My teeth tugged at my bottom lip, and I watched as his eyes were immediately drawn to the movement. Could he *please* stop looking at me like that?

"Besides doing a good deed for the holiday?"

"I'm all good-deeded out for the week, actually. My karma is in tip-top shape."

He smiled, and the sight almost had me handing over my ticket on the spot. I must seriously be losing it because no way should a complete stranger be having this sort of effect on me.

His chuckle sounded off again. "Anyone ever tell you you're hilarious?"

I shrugged. "It's been mentioned once or twice."

"Aight, how about this? Whatever you order up there is on me. Your ticket, my paper."

Watching to see if he was serious, I tapped a pointed nail against my lip as I fidgeted with one of the gold rings adorning the fingers on my other hand. My affinity for gold didn't just go as far as seeing it on fine ass men.

Thinking over his proposal wasn't as hard as I was trying to make it seem. Turning down a man when he was offering to spend some money, even if it was just on groceries, was just something I was not prepared to do. Why spend mine when I could spend his?

"See, you should've just led with that," I said with a smile just as one of the teenagers behind the counter called out number seventy-eight. "I wouldn't be me if I turned down a well-earned treat."

He didn't say a word, just stepped slightly to the side and allowed me to lead the way to the stall. Just when I decided to be irritated at the way the little boy immediately deferred to Golds for the order, it quickly vanished when he made sure to let me place mine first. I rattled off my short list, going extra heavy on the sweet potatoes. After making sure all the produce picked was up to my standards, I turned to my grocery benefactor for the day, which he took as his cue it was his turn. Once everything was all said and done, he let our little helper know how to bag the items before sliding a card out of his wallet and handing it over.

"I sort of wish I had another stop to make just to see how far your generosity goes," I giggled, grabbing my bags.

Before I could even get a good hold on them, he took them out of my hands. "Nah, ain't no way you finna be carrying these bags with me standing here." I threw up my hands, not about to argue with him. "And as far as my generosity, point out where you need to go, and we can head over and get what you need."

A barely restrained smile spread across my lips. "The gesture is greatly appreciated, but I've already done my rounds a few times and unfortunately, they don't have anything else I was hoping to grab. Honestly, this whole shopping day has worn me out, so I'm probably just going to head home."

He nodded. "Cool. Let's go."

I looked at him in surprise. "Thought you had plans?"

"Yeah, but what does that have to do with me walking you to your car to help you put these away?" he asked, gesturing to my stuff. His question was met with silence since I didn't really have an answer.

"Exactly."

We fell into step next to one another, making quick work of the maze of shoppers and heading out the front door.

"So, either you love sweet potatoes or you're on some special diet or some shit." He lifted the two bags as we came closer to my truck. "Because I ain't never seen somebody clean up like you just did."

"Please," I laughed. "All of those are not for me, though with the luck I had today, they might need to be since it doesn't look like I'm going to be eating shit else."

"Spending Thanksgiving by yourself?" He shook his head as I nodded. "Something's wrong with your ass, ain't it?"

"What?!" My shriek caught the attention of damn near everyone in the vicinity. Not paying them any mind, I came to a stop two cars away from mine. "Excuse you?" That attitude I was faking earlier was very real now.

"No disrespect, ma. Just looking for a reason as to why someone as funny and fine as you would be spending Thursday alone. Usually shit like that means you got enough red flags to fill a football field."

"Or maybe," I said, snatching two out of my three bags

from his grasp, "it means I just don't want to deal with anyone else's bullshit."

He didn't seem worried about my attitude at all as he chuckled while I stormed toward my car. It was time to go before I really cussed his ass out. He didn't know me well enough to try and carry me like that, little grocery treat be damned.

Popping the trunk and dropping the bags in, I turned and placed a hand on my hip. "Thanks for the help. Could've done without the insults, though, so please drop my shit in the back and go handle whatever business it is you need to take care of."

Not paying me any mind, he took the few strides he needed to place the last bag in the trunk. I slammed it shut, barely missing his fingers and not really giving a fuck. It would've served him right to get his hand caught. He must have found the entire thing hilarious because all he did was chuckle in response and start rubbing his damn jaw once again. As I turned to get into the car, he caught my hand in his.

"I'm not sure what about these last few minutes makes you think I want you touching me but…" My words trailed off as I looked at where our hands were joined and back up at him. Letting my hand go, he took a step back.

"I wasn't trying to offend you, thick mama. Just making an observation." That damned tongue snaked out again, and this time I knew he did it on purpose. It was not going to work. Well…not much.

"Yeah, well, intent versus impact. So, while your astute observation may have seemed harmless to you, it actually sounded really fucking rude to me."

"And that's on me. My apologies."

Maybe I was taking his comment a little too seriously. Shit, it was possible I was feeling more sensitive about spending Thanksgiving alone than I originally thought. Admittedly, that wasn't his fault, but was I about to say any of that to him? Hell no. We didn't even know each other's names yet here he was, judging the shit out of me. He could kiss my whole ass.

Just as I was getting ready to tell him that, he reached into his pocket, pulling out a small wad of cash. Peeling off a couple bills, he held them out toward me.

"What's this for?" I'd never turned my nose up at money, but there was a first time for everything.

"Just something slight for helping me out in there." When I didn't say anything in return, he took another step forward, apparently not at all worried about my reaction to his close presence. His entire aura was intoxicating, even when I didn't want it to be. He held the folded bills, a couple of hundreds from the look of them, up just a bit higher. "And my way of putting a cherry on top of my apology. It ain't my business to judge how you choose to spend your time. And judging it damn sure won't get me your number."

I smirked despite myself. As far as apologies went, this one wasn't too bad. Quickly making my decision, I took the money and leaned in close. Thanks to our similar heights, we were nearly eye-to-eye. Looking directly at him, I whispered, "I already told you. It's seventy-eight," before turning, making my way to the driver's side door, and climbing in. His perfect gold smile was the last thing I saw as I pulled off.

By the time I made it to the next traffic light, his words were still running on a loop in my mind. Pushing a few buttons on my display, I scrolled through my call log until the name I'd been searching for appeared. It only took a few rings for her voice to fill my car speakers.

"Hey, baby," answered Ms. Hazel.

"Are you sure Von won't be there?" Screw the small talk. We needed to cut right to the chase. Any other time, she would've chewed me out for not giving her a greeting, but today she was giving me a pass.

"Positive."

With a sigh, she finally pulled the answer out of me she'd been wanting for the last week. "Okay. What time should I be there on Thursday?"

CHAPTER THREE

SHORTY FROM THE MARKET REALLY HAD ME STUCK. THAT little attitude she called herself having only made her ten times finer to me. She was bad as fuck, standing damn near eye-to-eye with me, thick all over with a pretty ass face, plump lips, and a gold nose ring that glistened whenever the light hit it. I was a sucker for a woman with a short haircut. Shit, part of me wanted to get the name and number of her barber because the cut she was rocking was one of the cleanest I'd ever seen.

I'd felt her eyes on me as soon as she turned them in my direction. While my mind might have been occupied listening to my homeboy rattle off the list I'd left at my mom's house, my body was standing at full attention for her. She had my head spinning so much that by the time the call ended, I couldn't remember a damn thing he'd said to me, which left me no choice but to text him and have him send me a picture of the list.

Either shorty was mesmerized or she had absolutely no

shame because her eyes never left me. So, never one to let an opportunity pass me by, I decided to step to her on some easy shit. I should've known the combination of our attitudes would send the conversation downhill.

Once she snapped on me and made it clear she'd take my hand off if I didn't get out of her way, I could've charged it. Instead, I found myself digging in my pocket and sliding her a few bills. Money wasn't a thing for me, but handing it out randomly wasn't my MO either, yet she pulled it out of me without any hesitation or real attempt.

"So you managed to catch her attention, tricked off on ole girl a little bit, and still didn't get her name or her number?" Kal snickered as he helped me finish putting away the groceries.

"It's not *that* funny." His reaction had me feeling like I should've just kept the shit to myself.

"Maybe not to you, but the shit is comical to me." Closing the fridge, he added, "And you have nobody to blame but yourself because why would any of that even come out of your mouth?"

"You know I just be saying shit," I groaned, leaving the kitchen and ending up out on the back porch. I knew Kal wasn't too far behind me.

"Yeah, and as usual, the shit backfired." He pulled up a seat next to me and reached in his pocket, pulling out a pre-rolled blunt.

In the time it took for him to light it and take a few pulls, I ran through what happened in my head again. Shorty looked so fucking good in that leggings and hoodie combo, there was no doubt in my mind anything she wore would stop me in my tracks. The way she was quick on her feet and plenty of mouth drew me to her, too.

Mild-mannered, soft-spoken women who faded into the background had never been my ministry. Whatever I dished out, I wanted her to give back ten times over. If I was talking shit, whoever I was dealing with needed to be able to match that energy, whether it was directed toward me or whoever was in the vicinity. My shorty being able to hold her own against any person in any room turned me the fuck on.

"You act like pissing her off was my plan. I honestly thought she'd think the shit was funny." He passed me the blunt, and I took a pull, letting the smoke fill my lungs and calm me down. Neither of my parents really cared if I smoked when I came to visit, but my father had a hard line about smoking in the house. Thirty years grown or not, I was not fucking with him, even if it was colder than a motherfucka out here.

"My point is, yo' ass didn't actually have a plan. You thought you could just pull her 'cause you caught a vibe. Hate to break it to you, nigga, but you really ain't that charming."

My only response was to flip him off, which of course he found funny as hell. I really should've left his ass in North Carolina instead of bringing him home with me.

"You talking a lot of shit right now, but we'll see how much you got to say when the Stallions beat the Panthers' ass on Thursday," I said, changing the subject to the Thanksgiving Day football games. Even though there were three football teams within the vicinity of Acacia Hills, I'd always chosen to root for the Oakwood Stallions as opposed to DC or Baltimore's teams.

"Boy, the only way they're doing that is with a hope and a prayer."

"We'll see."

The two of us spent the next few hours smoking and talking shit, but thick mama from the market was never too far from my mind. If I got the opportunity to run into her again, no way in hell was I gonna waste it.

CHAPTER FOUR

sinna

From the minute I'd arrived at Ms. Hazel's house, she'd made it a point to keep me busy. Even though almost everyone coming was supposed to bring a dish, Hazel didn't trust anyone else to make the turkey wings, greens, or cornbread, so she always made them herself. I didn't mind helping her, though, which she knew. So, instead of relaxing with the rest of the guests and watching the Thanksgiving Day Parade, I spent my time in the kitchen. At least this was the perfect way to avoid any conversation around Von.

You wouldn't have to worry about avoiding the topic of your ex if you'd stayed your ass home instead of trying to prove a point to a nigga you probably won't ever see again.

Catiya's voice came through in my mind loud and clear, more than likely because she'd said the same exact thing to me two hours ago when I'd first pulled up in front of Mama Hazel's house. And yes, maybe she was right, but we were long past that now and there was no taking it back. I just had to hope my peace continued to go undisturbed.

"Is that my big booty homegirl in my favorite auntie's kitchen?" an unnecessarily loud voice called out. Lennon's ass didn't know how to be on anything except a ten.

"You better stop all that hollering before your favorite auntie comes in here and goes upside your head," I giggled as he strutted into the kitchen.

He kissed his teeth and rolled his eyes before pulling me into a hug. "Chile, she would never. She reserves all acts of violence for her trifling ass son."

"I heard that. And watch your mouth!"

We both snickered because Ms. Hazel did indeed hear everything. Nothing ever got past her. Plenty of stories had been passed around about how whenever Vontae or any of the kids in the family had been up to something, she caught them each and every time.

"Anyway, I can't believe she convinced you to come." The smile he was wearing was contagious, but it suddenly dropped as he eyed me suspiciously. "Hold the fuck up. Are you two back together? Because I swear I told you the last time needed to be the la—"

"Calm down, calm down. No, Von and I are not back together, nor do I intend for us to get back together." Lennon had always been nothing but nice to me, even though he was one of the few people in the family who didn't actually endorse or approve of my relationship with his older cousin.

"I'm here because Mama Hazel wore me down about coming, and since I honestly didn't have other viable plans, I decided to take her up on the offer. The only thing that solidified me coming today was her promising me he would not be here."

"Hmph, that's news to me, but I'm very glad to hear it. Now we can catch up, show out, and you can slide me an extra slice of pie because I know you got that thang on you."

"Do you think she would've let me through the door if I didn't?" To prove my point, I gestured to the reusable grocery bags on the counter behind me. "The sweet potatoes are almost done roasting in the oven, which means you're just in time to take your place as my favorite sous chef."

His fake whining started immediately. "Do I have a choice?"

My side-eye appeared right on cue. "Cut the shit please because we both know you love this part."

Blowing me a kiss as he took off his jacket, he said, "What can I say? I live for the drama, just like the rest of my family."

Ain't that the fucking truth.

"Speaking of, tell me all the good shit. What's new with you? It's been forever since we've caught up, so I need to know who and what you've been doing." He shot me a mischievous glance as he washed his hands, then began taking my various seasonings out of the bags. "And don't you dare leave out who's going to be stuffing *you* before the night is over."

"Lennon!" I shrieked. "You really have no fucking sense." Half the shit out of his mouth was inappropriate, and the other half never made a lick of fucking sense. At this point, I should've been used to it, but he never ceased to have me in a fit of laughter or searching for the nearest exit.

"Don't try it, just answer the question."

"Sorry to burst your bubble, Lenny baby, but the only thing over here getting stuffed is a turkey, and honestly, not even that because you know Ms. Hazel only fucks with turkey wings." We both snickered, knowing how much the older woman hated the idea of cooking a whole turkey.

"Friend, that is…so sad."

I rolled my eyes even though he was right. It'd been months since I last had sex. I certainly wasn't going to tell him the last bit of sex in my life had come courtesy of his cousin, thanks to a drunken night and a very strategic "Hey, big head" text message four months ago. He'd initiated that little exchange, and being the weak ass bitch I was, I'd let him slide through the front door of my apartment and right into me.

Before the thought could stay planted in my mind for too long, a vision of gold fronts and locs took its place. "Well, actually…I did meet someone the other day."

"Ooop! Do tell."

While he pulled out the perfectly roasted sweet potatoes and helped me make space on the counter to begin mixing the ingredients, I filled Lennon in on my encounter with the fine ass man at the Amish market.

"Wait, so he paid for your shit and then slid you three hundred dollars as an apology? And you didn't get his name or give him your damn number?"

"Nope." I shook my head, mentally kicking my own ass for being so stubborn.

"Chile, you know what? Maybe it's for the best. Ain't no way you know what to do with all that man if you couldn't lock it down right then and there. And considering who your last man was, you probably used to weak sauce anyway."

"You do realize that weak sauce is a member of your family, right?"

"I said what I said."

Kissing my teeth, I shot him a look. "You always talking shit."

"It's what I do best. Well, and suck di—"

"Something is smelling real good up in this kitchen!"

Right on cue, Mama Hazel walked into the kitchen, eyeing Lennon like she knew he'd been about to say something he had no business saying with his mama and aunties in the vicinity.

"Lennon baby, you better not be in here distracting her while she's making these pies."

"Of course not, Auntie!" he said, feigning innocence.

"Mhmm, sure. I'll tell you one thing, you keep talking about my baby boy and you will be eating whatever concoction your mama decided to bring." Even though Aunt Rose was only supposed to bring non-food-related items, she'd still managed to sneak in something she claimed was apple pie.

Lennon paled at the threat and zipped his lips with an imaginary key. No one wanted to be subjected to that sort of threat, mama or not.

CHAPTER FIVE

PULLING UP IN FRONT OF THE HOUSE, IT LOOKED LIKE MOST people had already made it to my aunt's place, including my mom and pops. Knowing her, she was in there playing hostess with the mostest. With the size of her house and how seriously she took the holidays, it didn't really surprise me. Everybody loved my Aunt Hazel, and spending time at a function she was throwing never disappointed. To be honest, missing the last few was something I regretted, but dealing with her punk ass son? Yeah, I'd skip suffering through his bullshit every time.

"You sure your people cool with me crashing like this?" Kal asked after we'd both climbed out of the car and made our way onto the sidewalk.

"I told you, yeah." Nodding my head toward the door so he would follow my lead, I headed up the driveway. "Aunt Hazel has always been the more the merrier type. And with the amount of food always leftover at these damn things, they probably need an extra mouth to feed." Stopping just before making a move to ring the doorbell, I groaned. "Shit, actually, maybe I should've left your greedy ass at home. Won't be shit left on the table for anyone else by the time you get going."

The "Nigga, fuck you," he shot me caused me to snicker.

"I'm just joking. Sensitive ass."

Finally pressing the bell to let people know we were here, it only took a minute for someone to come and open the door.

"Well, as I live and breathe. I thought your mama was completely full of shit when she said you were coming to dinner. Damn it, boy, now I owe her ten dollars and an extra sweet potato pie." The woman of the hour shook her head as she stepped to the side. "Well, it's too late for you to disappear now. Bring your ass in here," she teased.

Even while fussing, Hazel pulled me into a hug. I'd never tell my mama this, but Aunt Hazel's hugs were easily the best in the family. No matter how mad she may be at someone, no matter how upset the person on the receiving end might be, no matter what the fuck may have been going on in the world, everything always got better whenever Hazel wrapped you up in her arms. As little as her five foot four self was, she always managed to make me feel like a kid again when we were like this.

"My bad, Auntie. I'm sure you have an extra Patti pie around here though to give her."

"If that's the pie she was after, then I wouldn't be about to spend the next couple of hours hearing her gloat. The bet was for one of Sinna's pies," she huffed, letting me go.

I must've looked as confused as I felt because she added, "You'll understand when you taste a piece. I have no clue what that child does to those pies, but I swear if there was only one slice left, everyone in here would be ready to have a cage match over it. She's in the kitchen now with Lennon, whipping them up."

Well, at least now I knew why it smelled so good in here. Making quick work of introducing Kal, it seemed my presence was no longer a secret when other family members filed into the hall to see who'd shown up.

"Hey, baby. I told you, Hazel!" mama said as she pulled me into her own hug after I finished dapping up my pops. We'd missed each other since Kal and I had gone out to grab breakfast this morning.

"Yeah, Vera, I see his big ass, damn. You'll get your pie," Aunt Hazel snapped at her.

"Don't be a sore loser. I already know Sinna is in there right now making her favorite would-be mother-in-law her own pie, too."

"Y'all really in here trippin' over some pie?" This shit was wild to me. I racked my brain to figure out why the name was so familiar. "Sinna...ain't that Von's girlfriend?" Having never actually met shorty, I couldn't place a face with the name.

My face turned up in irritation. "Didn't you tell me he wasn't going to be here?" My plan had always been to come to dinner this year since I'd missed the last couple, but the prospect of not having to deal with Vontae had its advantages.

"Ex-girlfriend," my mother stage-whispered. "That child went and did something to mess it up." She shook her head. "And what I said was, who knows what the boy was doing? Hazel was real cagey when I asked her about it. It must be true, though, since Sinna is here, and I can't imagine she'd be willing to show up after their messy breakup. Won't hear me complaining, though. Especially not since if she hadn't shown up, Rose was going to try and be slick and recreate her sweet potato pie. Bad enough she brought some fake apple one up in here." She shook her head in disgust before walking off, more than likely to find the sister in question.

If he wasn't going to be here and him and ole girl had broken up, then what was she here for? Maybe she was hoping he'd show up. Didn't shorty have her own family to spend the holidays with? Ain't no way you'd find me hanging with any of my exes' families for shits and giggles. To each their own, though.

After finishing up hellos, it looked like out of all the people here, the only ones Kal and I hadn't come across were Lennon and this mysterious ass Sinna. Remembering they were supposed to be in the kitchen, we made our way there. Lennon was nowhere to be found. What we did find, though, was the thickest ass known to man bent over in front of the fridge.

"Goddamn," Kal muttered next to me, and I had to fucking agree. The chocolate sweater dress she was wearing was just long enough to cover her ass, but if she arched any more...

"Girl, Auntie said sh—" The sound of Lennon's voice snapped my attention away from what was in front of me to the other entrance into the kitchen. He stared at me with a knowing smirk on his face. "I see you in here putting on a show for the niggas, friend."

"What are you talking about?"

That voice. Fuck, I knew that voice. I'd been thinking about it since its owner left me standing in the parking lot of the Amish market a couple days ago. Sure enough, the face that matched the raspy voice and ass for days was the very one that had me about to make a habit of hitting up the market just for a chance to see her again.

"Damn, thick mama. If you wanted to see me again, all you had to do was say so."

CHAPTER SIX

sinna

"Hold up, Gideon is Golds?!"

"Lower your damn voice!" I hissed, snatching up Lennon's arm. As soon as my brain caught up with my eyes and ears and the reality that one of the newcomers in the kitchen was one I was slightly familiar with, my thigh-high boots had nearly came off my feet with how fast I grabbed Lennon and ran up out of the kitchen. We slipped through the first door I could find, which happened to be a hall bathroom.

"Uh-uh, girl, don't be manhandling me just 'cause you about to get caught hopping from cousin dick to cousin dick. It's a good thing I don't like coochie, or we'd all be in trouble."

"Fuck you." I loved Lennon, but he was dangerously close to getting the shit smacked out of him if he kept playing with me.

"Too soon? My bad," he giggled even though if you asked me, wasn't shit about this situation funny.

"How the hell was I supposed to know who he was or

that he'd show up here? I've never even met Gideon before today. Or Tuesday, I guess." There hadn't been many of Von's family events I'd missed over the last couple of years, and not once had the beautiful man out there been on my radar.

"You sure? 'Cause I could've sworn..." His words trailed off, and I could only assume it was because he was scrolling through his mental calendar. "Damn, you might actually be right." Taking a second to lean against the sink behind him, Lennon crossed his arms over his chest. "Makes sense, I guess. I mean it's not like Gids lives in the area anymore. He's been in North Carolina for what, like four or five years now? So I guess he does tend to miss most of the shit we do around here. Well, either that or he purposely shows up when he knows Von won't be there."

Nodding, I took in everything he said. It wasn't a secret Von didn't get along with Gideon, though anytime I asked why, he never really gave me an actual answer. He always seemed to get irritated whenever the question would come up, so I just stopped asking after a while. With Von's personality and how spoiled he tended to act, his cousins weren't the only people who couldn't stomach being around him for too long. His attitude could grate the nerves of even the holiest of saints. Two years with him was two years too long, so twenty-seven years of dealing with his bullshit? Yeah, I completely understood.

Lennon's next question snapped me out of my whirl-wind of thoughts. "And you never saw a picture of him? Like not even one?"

An exasperated sigh left my chest. "Maybe like one or two, but he certainly didn't look like *that* in either of them!" Whatever pictures had been scattered through the family photo albums I'd seen occasionally in no way did the chocolate god in the other room justice. The years had certainly been good to him because the boy in the college graduation picture that came to mind had filled out, found his way, and become a certified man.

Groaning, I leaned back, hitting my head against the bathroom wall with more force than intended, which meant an even bigger headache was probably in my future. "I am so fucked."

"And you call me dramatic." Lennon rolled his eyes. "Calm down, friend. It's not like you and him even did anything. A little flirting never hurt anybody."

Apparently, we'd reached the part of the conversation where we were going to just ignore how I mentioned fantasizing about putting my pussy on his sideburns. Cool, got it.

"Besides, things could be a lot worse. Imagine if Vontae was here."

No. I refused to imagine it because the universe could not be that cruel.

CHAPTER SEVEN

"So how long do you plan on ignoring me?"

If the way her shoulders stiffened was any sort of tell, she'd heard me. Apparently, I wasn't going to get an answer, though, because she went right back to mixing whatever she had going on in her little bowl. Just as stubborn as she'd been the other day. Good.

Chuckling, I pulled out one of the barstools at the island and sat down. "Damn, if I've got you this shook, it must mean you've been thinking about me extra hard, huh?"

"Don't flatter yourself."

And there was that attitude I'd been craving. The shit was just as sexy as it'd been the first time she'd turned it on me. Shorty still wasn't trying to look at me, which was fine. It just gave me more time to get my fill of looking at her. She had the same gold stud in her nose and gold rings on her fingers she'd been wearing when we first met. The way they looked against her skin, especially combined with her chocolate off-the-shoulder dress… My lil' thick mama was looking good as fuck.

"Not you trying to match my swag already, ma." Just like I thought, my teasing got her attention as her eyes snapped up toward me in irritation. A smirk formed on my face at the thought.

"You wish," she scoffed, which only pulled a full-blown smile out of me. Her eyes immediately dipped low enough I knew she was staring directly at my golds, just the way I wanted her to. It'd drawn her to me the first time we'd seen each other. Hopefully, it would have the same effect again.

"Glad to see you haven't gotten over that little staring problem of yours after all. Had a nigga missing having your eyes on him and shit."

She rolled her eyes, but whether she knew it or not, it was obvious the wall she'd tried to put up was breaking down. The way her posture relaxed and the edge of her mouth tipped up just enough in the promise of a smirk told me everything I needed to know.

"Conceited much?"

"Maybe. If I say yes, does it earn me a favor?" This time, her lips didn't play at a smile but gave me an actual one instead. "Shit, never mind. That's what I wanted to see right there."

Finally putting the spoon down, she braced herself against the island and looked at me full-on. "Did you know you're a pain in the ass?"

"Your boyfriend may have made mention of it once or twice."

Her smile dropped as she narrowed her eyes. "Ex-boyfriend." After a slight pause, she added, "Which I'm sure you already know."

"Just checking to see if my sources knew what they were talking about or if they're just as full of shit as he is."

Another smile, though she tried to hide it this time.

"Sinna…" Just tasting her name on my tongue did something to me.

"Gideon…" she countered. Hearing my name come from hers was better.

"I think I might love the way you say my name even more than your little attitude. And that's saying a lot because I haven't been able to stop thinking about it since you drove off on me the other day."

"What are you, a sucker for punishment?"

"Nah, I just love a beautiful woman who has some bite to her."

"Beautiful woman, huh?" A smirk appeared on her lips. "At least you clearly have good taste."

And that right there. Knowing she looked the fuck good and making sure everyone else knew it too? That sort of confidence was what made me want to snatch her up and let everything that had run through my mind recently play out like a motherfucking movie.

"At least now I can stop calling you Golds in my head." The words left her lips and she immediately sealed them, eyes going wide. Clearly she hadn't meant to let that slip, but it was too late now. My attention was focused right on her.

"So you have been thinking about me. Gave me a nickname and everything." *Golds.* Yeah, I could get used to her calling me that. Shit, she could call me whatever she wanted as long as she called me, for real.

"It doesn't mean anything, trust me. I just needed to have something to call you when I told the story of how a nigga conned his way into my grocery pickup and tricked off on me before pissing me off so bad, I left him standing stuck and clueless."

Chuckling, I shook my head. "Smart ass mouth." She shrugged, and it only encouraged what I said next. "That's cool. It just means I get to make up a nickname for you for when I tell folks about the shorty I mesmerized so bad at the market, she pulled up on me at my auntie house on some stalker shit, just to spend the holiday with me."

"There you go with that bullshit," she said, the sound of her kissing her teeth making my grin go even wider.

"Yeah, there I go." Pausing, I contemplated my next question. *Fuck it.* I needed to know. "You really had no clue who I was at the market?"

Even though the two of us never met, it was sort of wild to think we were both completely unaware of the other person. Shit, even if I had known who she was, it wouldn't have stopped where my mind was going. Family or not, ain't no fucking way I could be loyal to a nigga who wasn't loyal to me. And even if I was going to stick to a code for my cousin, something told me a chance with Sinna was a once-in-a-lifetime opportunity. Twice, it seemed, in my case. If that nigga didn't know what to do with her, I sure as hell did.

"Not one bit. This probably comes as no surprise, but you weren't really a topic of discussion in my relation-ship." Turning away from me, she went to the fridge and grabbed a carton of eggs and maple syrup. "Hope that wasn't a blow to your ego."

"Nah, not at all. Especially since after today, you won't remember a time when a nigga wasn't on your mind."

"Inflated egos must be a family trait. If you don't have shit else in common with Von, y'all sure have that."

"Respectfully, thick mama, don't ever in your life compare me to that weak ass nigga." Standing up and making my way around the island until I was standing right in front of her, I made sure to add, "Real always recognizes real, and he's never looked familiar."

There was never a time when Vontae didn't irritate the fuck out of me. It didn't matter whether two days or two years had passed since we last saw each other.

Sitting her supplies down on the island, she looked at me, slightly cocking her head to the side. "My bad. I'd say no offense meant, but we both know I'd be lying." Her beautiful smile appeared, and it drew me even closer to her.

"And we both know I don't mind. Just make sure you don't put me in the same category as him again."

"Duly noted."

"Now my name and yours?" My hand reached out and cupped her chin as I leaned in just enough. "You can put us together any time you want."

Pulling her bottom lip between her teeth, her eyes bored into mine. "Also duly noted."

CHAPTER EIGHT

gideon

No one could ever accuse my family of being quiet. During our little kitchen standoff, the sounds of whatever football game was on along with the bets, taunts, and laughter carried through the house, breaking us out of the world we'd found ourselves in. As much as I wanted to test out this shit between us and set off the live wire it was clear we both felt, I took a step back and let her slip out of my hold as reality set in. I wasn't too worried. If I had my way, this wouldn't be our only opportunity to make that shit happen.

"I can't believe Aunt Hazel let you commandeer her kitchen. You do realize no one cooks here except for her, don't you?"

A glint appeared in her eye like she knew something I didn't. Shit, maybe she did. As far as I knew, anyone bringing an actual food dish to Thanksgiving dinner had to cook it at their own home because Hazel's kitchen was strictly off-limits. It was her domain, the place where no one else even dared question or challenge her. The rest of us were lucky to just be able to pass through it. Clearly, though, within the last couple of years, something had changed.

"All you need to know is I have special privileges." Cocky, but I both loved and respected it since I was the same way.

"Would that have anything to do with this pie I keep hearing about? The one my mama and auntie were taking bets and ready to fight over?"

The laugh she gave me captured her raspy voice perfectly, forcing me to bite back a groan. "Maybe."

"Nah, you've got to give me more than that. And while you're at it, how about you toss in how you went from spending the holiday by yourself to spending it with this wild ass family of mine? 'Cause if I recall, you said something about not wanting to put up with anyone else's bullshit."

Something about the way she narrowed her eyes and quirked her lips up to the side in annoyance made me want to poke at her every chance I got. "You know, you're cute as fuck when you're trying to act like I'm getting on your nerves."

"Who says I'm acting? You are absolutely irritating as hell."

"You'll learn to love it." *I'll make sure of it.* "Don't change the subject though."

Poking her lip out just a little, shorty measured out a bit of maple syrup before pouring it into the mixture she'd gone back to working on. "I don't want to say."

The last thing I wanted to do was make her uncomfortable. For all the teasing and shit we were doing, overstepping boundaries was never my thing. If this really was something she didn't want to talk about, I'd leave it alone. Reaching out to cover her hand with mine, I said as much.

Sighing and shaking her head, she said, "You know, you shouldn't be able to be fine as hell while also being sweet and funny. Matter of fact, I think it might be illegal."

"Wouldn't be my first run in with the law, ma."

"Of course not," she chuckled. "Grab the bourbon out of the purple bag?"

Taking a quick look around, it didn't take long for me to figure out which bag she was referring to. Bourbon in sweet potato pie was new shit for me, but maybe that was why everyone was so pressed about having a slice.

"Basically, spending the holidays with my family just wasn't appealing even though I had all intentions of trying to go that route. Coming here also wasn't an option for obvious reasons." Vontae had to be the reason she was referring to. "But Hazel is like a mama to me, and I hate disappointing her. That, coupled with the shit you gave me at the market the other day about red flags and whatnot. I guess I didn't want to let mama down, but I also didn't want to prove you right."

Damn. I hadn't meant to be heavy-handed with shorty, but if it worked out in my favor, then who was I to complain or contradict it? Instead of dwelling on our previous conversation, which would only kill the vibe, I did what I seemed to do best around her: crack jokes.

"In that case, you're welcome." Her ass was ready to let me have it until she saw my teasing grin.

"Again, on my damn nerves." This time though, we were both laughing.

"Okay then, since we've established my talented ass mouth is why your fine ass is gracing me with your presence today, back to the matter at hand. Why is everyone so pressed about this pie? What's the secret? It's the bourbon, isn't it?"

"First, it's not really a secret. Second, the bourbon is part of it. Brown liquor makes everything better if you ask me, so obviously the rule should apply to food, too." A woman who loved bourbon as much as I did? Yeah, she was finna have me gone over her ass.

"The other not-so-secret ingredient is extra cinnamon because it's just my favorite. You get a little extra spice, and it makes it smell more amazing than usual." Her eyes flickered up to meet mine. "And of course, I give it my special touch and love."

I turned what she said over in my head as she added the very ingredient she'd just mentioned. There was one particular thing she'd said that flipped the switch on my inner light. "A little extra cinnamon for Sinnamon, huh?"

She paused, spice shaker held firmly in her hand as she narrowed her eyes at me. "Don't you dare."

"Too late." I shot her my signature toothy grin. "Looks like I just found your nickname...Sinnamon."

"Nooooo," she groaned, putting the spice she now shared a name with back down. "My name isn't even spelled with a *C*." Giving the bowl another couple of whisks to blend the latest additions, she shot me a pleading look.

"And that's fine. Sinnamon with an *S* is even sexier."

"It's a stripper's name."

"And what do you have against strippers? It's good, honest work. Show me a lazy stripper, and I'll show you someone who ain't getting paid."

Not nearly as irritated as she wanted me to think she

was, she traded the whisk for a ladle, apparently ready to start filling the empty pie crusts in front of her. I was so busy being pleased with myself, I almost missed her mumbling, "At least it's better than Sinner."

I barked out a laugh. "Who the fuck was calling you *Sinner*?"

"Von's dumbass friends." I opened my mouth, but much to my pleasure, she beat me to the punch. "I know. Don't compare you to that nigga or his friends, right?"

"Exactly."

With a playful roll of her eyes, she slid her big bowl toward me. "Here, make yourself useful, Golds, and help me fill up the next batch of pie shells."

"I got you, Sinnamon."

CHAPTER NINE

sinna

FIVE PIES LATER, IT WAS FINALLY TIME TO GET THE FIRST round of dinner going. Despite my initial shock, seeing and spending time with Gideon—or Golds as I'd decided to still call him since that gorgeous grill of his was once again on display—had made the day infinitely better. After Lennon conveniently disappeared, spouting some bullshit about me finding a more than suitable replacement anyway, it turned out he was right. Gideon was very good at taking direction and keeping me busy.

Thankfully, if anyone else thought it was weird he was spending time with me in the kitchen instead of watching the game or catching up with his family, no one made mention of it. There were also no mentions of Vontae or our breakup either once we did finally rejoin the group. I had the sneaking suspicion the subject had been deemed off-limits by Mama Hazel, at least long enough for everyone to ensure they got the pie they wanted.

Speaking of mama…

"Everybody ready to say the blessing?" she asked,

though every person at the table knew it wasn't an actual question. If you weren't ready, you had thirty seconds to get ready.

Just like they did every year, the kids had their own table situated in the sunroom while the adults filled two tables in the formal dining room. I'd gotten lucky and wound up at the table with the usual suspects: Hazel, Rose and her husband Jackson, Vera and her husband Dennis, and Lennon, along with Golds' plus-one, Kal, and the man himself, who happened to be sitting directly across the way trying to play footsies with me.

I was so busy trying not to laugh, I missed it when someone called his name. And apparently, he did too.

"My bad, auntie. What'd you say?"

"I said," she repeated while her eyes darted between the two of us suspiciously, "since you're gracing us with your presence, it seems only fitting for you to grace us with prayer, too."

He gave her a swift nod as we all bowed our heads.

"Bless the hands that prepared this food, and please bless us as we enjoy it. I'd like to give thanks for the ability to be amongst family today. I don't always get to do this as much as I should or wish, but please know I'm thankful for each and every person at this table, especially the new faces that will hopefully become real familiar."

As he said the last line, I peeked through my lids and saw him looking directly at me. What type of nigga used prayer to flirt? My type of nigga, honestly.

"Thank you, baby." Clasping her hands together, Mama Hazel looked around eagerly, clearly not put off by his last words. "Y'all already know how this goes. Grab a dish, take a scoop, pass it around. Let's fill these plates up!"

She didn't have to tell anyone twice. Both tables fell into a rhythm while we all served ourselves, ready to dig in. Feeling eyes on me as I grabbed a spoonful of green beans, my own gaze lifted and immediately met with Gideon's. He gave me a wink, making me roll my eyes in response, even though we both knew I thought the shit was cute.

"So, Sinna..." He paused slightly, and I had a sneaking suspicion he was wondering if the nickname he'd given me earlier was good for use in mixed company. "When do we get to taste these world-famous pies?"

He was really trying to be slick like I hadn't told him in the kitchen he'd be lucky to even get a taste at all. It all depended on whether or not he was on his best behavior during dinner. "Who says—"

The sound of the front door chime cut me off as it filled the room. My eyes briefly looked at the empty chair next to me. The one I hadn't thought to question or pay much attention to until now.

"Mama?" There was a question in my tone, which quickly changed to irritation when I looked up to find her looking at me with a guilty expression.

You've got to be fucking kidding me.

Across from me, Gideon looked just as irritated as I felt. Everyone else seemed to focus their attention on me, trying to gauge my reaction as a familiar voice yelled from the hall. The entire room fell into silence. Hell, even the kids' table was reduced to whispers. I really should've gone with my first mind and stayed my ass home because this was about to be some bullshit.

"Ma, sorry I'm late, but—"

That baritone stopped in its tracks, and it wasn't hard to imagine how his face probably looked. He couldn't see my face since my back was to the dining room entrance, but how many other bald-headed blondes did he know? Last time I checked, none. So it was safe to say seeing me sitting at his mama's dining room table today was the last thing he expected, despite the fact that for the last couple of years, me being there was a regular occurrence.

The silence seemed to stretch forever before it was finally broken.

"I should've known," his mother said, standing. I don't think I've ever seen Hazel as nervous as she seemed to be right now. The way she was actively avoiding eye contact with me deserved to be put into a master class. "You can never be on time for anything, honestly," she said with a tsk.

"Yeah, well, we had to make a stop first," he said cautiously. I heard each one of his footsteps as he walked to the head of the table to pull his mother into a hug and place a kiss on her temple.

Unable to avoid it any longer, his eyes moved to meet mine. No one could ever accuse Von of not being fine, though sometimes an argument could be made that his attitude knocked him back a few notches. Still, with his fresh fade, clear bronze skin, and slightly muscular frame, he was nothing to sneeze at. He knew it too. It pissed me off, actually.

"Hey, Sin."

Something in the way he said my name put me on edge. He was fidgeting, which he only did when he had something to hide or was doing something he knew he had no business doing. It didn't make sense, though, because if anyone was out of place here, it was me, not him.

"Hi, Von."

"Vontae baby, it's so good to see you. We didn't know you were coming," Vera said as he slid around his mother and gave his aunt a kiss. His eyes were so focused on me, he completely missed the nervous look she gave Gideon. Actually, he didn't seem to notice his cousin at all. "Umm…did I hear you say, '*we* had to make a stop'?"

It took a second or two to register, but now that she mentioned it…

"Uhhh, yeah," he said, rubbing the back of his neck, eyes darting from her to me. "I know we usually have extra, so I didn't think it'd be a problem if I brought somebody."

Ain't this about a bitch. So, not only had I been bamboozled into showing up here today—because at this point, I was sure that's what Ms. Hazel had done—but now I was faced with both my ex and his new flavor of the month? The chances his "guest" wasn't a woman were slim to none. And you know what, that was his prerogative. This was his mama's house, and he could bring whoever he wanted around here. I was the one who didn't belong.

Right on cue, a slim, short, fair-skinned girl with an abundance of curly hair—in other words, the total opposite of me—came into view. "Baby, you know I have short legs and can't keep up when you move so fast."

Wow.

"Sorry, babe," Von said as she made her way to him, pressing herself against his side. He wrapped an arm around her, sending her his signature smile, the one he used to make anyone within a ten-mile radius swoon. Somehow, looking at it now, it just didn't do it for me anymore. Not after I'd been introduced to the smile covered in gold.

"Everyone, this is Evie. Evie, this is everyone." Vontae went around the tables, letting her know who everyone was. When he got to Gideon, finally noticing his presence, I watched his jaw flex. Once he made it around to me, it seemed he'd recovered from the shock of seeing me and was probably about to switch into asshole mode.

"And this is Sinna, my ex, and apparently still a very special dinner guest."

"Oh, umm…hi," Evie said sheepishly.

"Yeah, Sinna tends to…" He paused, and I knew whatever he said next was going to make me want to smack him. "Stick around and hover, sort of like your favorite puppy."

"*Excuse—*"

"Why don't y'all have a seat?" Hazel said, knowing I was two seconds away from jumping in her son's shit. "I'm sure we can make some room at the table."

"I'll go ahead and move over with Yvette and them," Gideon's dad said, standing and grabbing his plate. "Y'all know I like to talk shit to Evan about the Ravens anyway."

"Perfect, and then Von can take the seat next to…" Hazel looked over at me, and my only response was to give her a look. *Don't even try it.*

"Here!" Aunt Vera said. "I don't mind moving next to Sinna. Maybe I can actually get those pie measurements out of her this year."

"Nah, ma, you're good where you are. I'll keep Sinna company."

Gideon's words drew a reaction from his mother, me, Hazel, and Von all at once, the last one on the list looking the most irritated by the suggestion.

"I mean, I'm good sitting next to Sin. We can catch up," Von said.

"Nah, cuz. You worry about helping Miss Evie over there get straight." Gideon flashed her a smile, and apparently, it had the same effect on her that it did on me by the way she started blushing. "I got thick mama."

With the way Von's face turned up at the nickname, you would've thought he'd smelled the nastiest trash in existence. He clearly wanted to argue, but Gideon didn't leave any room for discussion, already getting up and relocating himself to my side of the table.

Sensing the mounting tension in the room, Hazel placed a smile on her face and said, "Sinna, baby, why don't you help me grab more green beans from the kitchen? We can check and see if those pies of yours have cooled down yet."

I stood without saying a word. We both knew it didn't matter if the pies had cooled down or not since we hadn't even gotten good into the actual meal yet, but clearly a conversation needed to be had. As my feet moved on autopilot to follow her out of the room, my emotions spiked, going all over the place. Confusion, anger, hurt, embarrassment. They all seemed to be swirling together, and not one wanted to give me a break.

We'd barely made it into the privacy of the kitchen before I whipped around and stared down into the eyes of the woman who I never thought would stoop this low. "You promised me. You specifically promised me he wouldn't be here!" The words escaped on a low hiss, but only because I didn't want anyone in the other room to hear what I had to say.

"I swear, I had no clue he was bringing someone with him, Sinna baby. He never mentioned anything about bringing that Evie girl."

"That is not the point, Ms. Hazel, and you know it." The hurt in her eyes at the use of her name instead of my usual term of endearment was almost enough for me to pull back a little. But like Brandy said, almost doesn't count.

"Did you think I was joking? Like I was playing hard to get when I said I didn't want to see him?"

She sighed, placing both hands on the kitchen island. "I thought maybe if I could get you two in one place, you'd both stop all this foolishness and see how much you two love each other. That you're perfect for one another."

My groan came through loud and clear while my fingers massaged my temples and my eyes closed. I wasn't nearly drunk enough for all this. Was it too early to break out the brown liquor? Technically, it'd already been cracked open, so there wasn't much to just grabbing a sip.

"Respectfully, mama, that is not your business, and it wasn't your decision to make." Finally able to look at her again, I added, "And all you've done at this point is put all of us in an awkward situation, me more than anyone else."

Here I was in a house that belonged to my ex-boyfriend's mama, with him and the rest of his family present because she decided she wanted to play match-maker. And as if that weren't bad enough, his new girl-friend had a front row seat, and so did his cousin. The cousin I had no clue was related to him and had been fantasizing about for the last two days. The universe really loved fucking with me. What had I done to deserve this type of karma?

"Admittedly, I might have overstepped a bit."

It was clear she expected me to absolve her and tell her it was okay, but I wasn't going to do that. So instead, we fell into an awkward silence. By the lack of noise coming from the other room, it didn't take a genius to figure out everyone in there was trying to hear our conversation. Fan-fucking-tastic.

"Maybe it's best if I just go."

"No! Please, Sinna baby, don't go." Grabbing my hand, she took a breath. "Just…stay. I know I didn't go about this the right way. I should've minded my business. You're just…you're like a daughter to me. The thought of losing you just wasn't something I was ready to face."

"Mama, the only way you'll lose me is if you pull something like this ever again." Whether she meant well or not, putting me in this position was the farthest thing from fair.

"You don't have to worry about that. I promise to mind my business from now on." Mhmm, we'd have to see how long that actually lasted. "Come back with me?"

Shaking my head, I took a step back. "I just need a minute." It was clear from the look she was giving me she expected me to sneak out of the back door as soon as she left the room. "If I decide to leave, which is still well within my rights, I promise to let you know first."

It wasn't hard to tell she wanted to say something else but seemed to think better of it because she just nodded, pulled me in for a quick hug, and headed back into the dining room.

It was time to weigh my options. On one end of the

spectrum, if I left now, everyone would know it was because of Von. They'd probably attribute it to me being jealous, which wasn't the case, but if it was one thing these people loved more than sweet potato pie, it was petty ass gossip and drama. The alternative, though, was suffering through this damn dinner, which would be infinitely worse.

So what was the solution to this extremely shitty scenario? In the end, it was an easy choice. Torturing myself by staying in a house with a person I had no desire to spend time with was not on the agenda for me. Taking my ass home was.

Decision made, I got myself together enough to go back in to say goodbye, only for an energy shift in the room to stop me in my tracks.

CHAPTER TEN

sinna

"FIGURED SOMEONE SHOULD COME AND CHECK ON YOU. Auntie is out there trying to…shit, I don't know, explain the situation without it being fucking awkward."

Do not turn around and look at him. "And how's it going?"

"Just as bad as you probably think that shit is," he snickered. "But at least it gave me the opportunity to come find you."

Every part of my body felt on edge as his steps came closer. I felt him. Knew the moment he was close even before I felt him pressed up against my back. Felt my knees almost give in to the temptation of going weak as he planted his hands on the counter on either side of mine, caging me in. With his breath against the back of my neck, my shoulders dipped, and a shiver ran down my spine. Before I could think better of it, the tension left my body and I leaned against his.

"You're not leaving me, are you, thick mama?" The

whispered words caressed my ears, and the warmth of it caused me to let out a small moan.

"I might've thought about it."

"Don't think too hard. I'd be extra offended if you left and I was stuck here with that asshole by myself."

"I'm sure he'd love that." This time when I laughed, he laughed along with me. Finally turning around to face him, I braced myself against the counter.

"So, what do I have to do to convince you to stay?"

My look had to let him know I was skeptical at best. "Somehow, I doubt you're persuasive enough for that."

"You sure?"

I meant to answer. I swear I did, only his fingers trailing under my dress and along my inner thigh distracted me before I could. "Wh-what do you think you're doing?"

"Just trying to be a little…" He leaned in, lips inches away from mine as the tips of his low-cut nails scraped against my skin. This time I didn't even try to stop the moan that found its way out of my throat. "Persuasive."

We were in the kitchen. A kitchen with two separate entrances anyone could walk through at any time, including the man I'd been dating just five months ago and his mother. Everything in me tried to remember that, and yet my mind went blank as soon as two of his fingers pressed against my covered pussy.

"Oooh, *fuck*." The first gasp was followed by another, then a whimper as my head fell back and my grip on the edge of the island tightened. The way Gideon made sure to skirt one nail so it scraped against the soaked fabric and my clit made my thighs shake and my chest quiver.

"Gideon."

"I love the way you say my name, Sinnamon." He did

it again, pressing harder this time so my panties were pushed into my wet, sticky heat, framing the most sensitive part of me. "But I think I want to hear you moan something else instead."

He nipped at the side of my lip, following it up with a trail of kisses along my jawline to my neck. "You know what I want to hear."

Gaining a bit of control over myself, one hand reached up, snaking itself into his locs. "Let me see them first." It wasn't a request, it was a command, and he took it as such, rewarding me with the vision of his bottom row of golds as he continued to rub my pussy.

"Golds," I gasped, closer and closer to detonating.

"Mmhmm. Just what I wanted." He leaned back in, lips brushing against my collarbone. "Now give me what else I want," he ordered against my skin. And I was ready to do just that when Von's voice snapped me out of my pre-orgasmic haze.

"Yeah, okay, ma. I'll let her know."

"Shit," I hissed, pushing Gideon back, my chest heaving. Kissing his teeth, he obliged, shooting an irritated look in the direction the voice had come from. Trying as best I could to not look like I hadn't just been about to come apart in the middle of the kitchen, I pulled myself together just enough to catch my breath as Von rounded the corner. God help me because the last thing I needed right now was to get stuck in the middle of a damn pissing contest between these two.

CHAPTER ELEVEN

gideon

"SIN, I—"

Whatever he'd been about to say died on his lips when he realized Sinna wasn't alone. This nigga had the worse timing. I had shorty just where I wanted her. A few seconds longer and my fingers would've been covered in her essence. By the look on his face, it was clear Von thought something was up, though there was no real way for him to know what. Even though I'd let her push me away, I ain't give her that much space, still sticking close enough that if the nigga would leave, we could finish what we started.

"Y'all taking a while in here, and ma said we can't start eating until everyone is back at the table. What's the holdup?"

"Nothing," she said, rolling my eyes. "Go—I mean Gideon was just helping me check on the pies. That's all." I smirked at her almost-slipup.

"And that takes both of y'all?"

"We got a lil' distracted, *that's all*. Wanted to make

sure shorty was good and then just tried to sneak a taste." Sinna's head whipped around to look at me, and I smirked. "Of the pies, I mean."

Von's eyes tracked us suspiciously, but I really wasn't worried about whatever he *thought* he was putting together.

"Yeah, well, I got it from here." His eyes left me and went straight to her, pissing me off. Who the fuck did he think he was? This nigga must be tripping if he really thought he still had a claim on her, especially after walking in here with another woman.

"Sin, I need to talk to you."

"Nah, she's good."

"What?" he asked, and Sinna just groaned lightly in response.

"I said, she's good. From where I'm standing, ain't really shit y'all got to talk about." Talking to him wouldn't just piss me off, it would ruin any chance of her staying for dinner.

Reaching out to nudge me, she shook her head. "Gideon, it's fine."

Von's face twisted in the way it always did when he was either confused or called himself being pissed off. They usually went hand in hand with him. "Wait, how the fuck y'all know each other?"

"Watch your mouth, lil' boy," Hazel snapped from the other room. That woman truly had bionic ears. It was the reason none of us kids ever got away with anything growing up.

"We know each other from knowing each other," I shrugged.

"Nigga, from what I hear, you've been in town all of

three days. The only way you'd know my girl is if you went looking for my girl."

"Who?!" Sinna asked, looking at him as if he'd grown three heads.

Puffing out his chest, he took a couple steps toward us. "You heard what the fuck I said, Sin."

Placing my hands on her hips, I moved shorty behind me to put a bit of distance between them. The way Von's eyes shifted told me he didn't miss the movement. Good.

"Nigga, I suggest you take that bass out your voice when you're talking to her. Matter of fact, just don't say shit to her at all. Worry about whoever you brought up in Auntie house cause Sinnamon over here? She's my concern."

"*Sinnamon*? What kinda weird ass nickname is that?"

"And again, you're worried about shit that really ain't your concern. Just go ahead and make your way back into the dining room. We'll be there in a minute."

Knowing my cousin, he wanted to say something else. Probably some smart shit that would have me ready to rock him, but instead, he kissed his teeth and backed away slowly. "Yeah, whatever." He focused his attention behind me. "We'll talk later, *Sin*. When we don't have an audience or a room full of people ready to eat."

My eyes didn't stop tracking him until he was fully out of the kitchen. Finally turning around, I found the woman in question looking at me with an amused expression. She clearly found this shit funny.

"I'm your concern now?" Her arms were crossed over her chest, only bringing more attention to how beautifully sculpted her body was.

"Ain't that what I said?" My arm wrapped around her

waist, pulling her body against mine. Fuck, I could feel my dick turning rock solid.

"It is, but I certainly don't remember saying that."

"You sure? I'm pretty sure I heard it."

"Did you, or was that the sound of your ego talking?"

My eyes narrowed. "You got jokes."

Giggling, she wrapped her arms around my neck. "Just a few." The way she leaned in and kissed me, lips enveloping mine, tongue licking across the seam, didn't do a damn thing to calm me or my dick down. My hands reached down, palming a handful of ass, causing her mouth to open on a gasp. I groaned, itching to pull her dress up and remove the barrier between us, but instead, I slowed the kiss and pulled away.

"Let's go, Sinnamon. I promise to get another taste later."

The fake pout she gave me was cute as hell, prompting me to drop one more kiss on her lips. Satisfied, she let me go and started to walk away. Unable to resist, I gave her ass a smack and chuckled at the squeak she let out. Her ass was mine. We just needed to get through dinner first.

Easier said than done. When Von said they were all waiting for us, I figured he was full of shit, and he was because everyone was already tearing up whatever they had out on their plates before he got there. Our absence must have been noticed, though, because several eyes tracked us when we entered the room, including his, Kal's, my mama's, and Aunt Hazel's.

Being the gentleman I was raised to be, I pulled Sinnamon's chair out before taking my own seat.

"Thank you."

"Anytime, sweetheart."

The sound of a throat clearing was obviously meant to take my attention away from her, but I was having too great of a time taking in her gorgeous face to give the owner the satisfaction. Not happy about being ignored, the throat cleared again.

"You should probably handle that. Maybe a glass of water will do the trick."

"Maybe I'm trying to figure out what's got you staring so hard. Or, you know, maybe you can just share what y'all spent so much time talking about in the kitchen."

"That's not actually your business, Vontae," Sinnamon responded as I passed her the platter of turkey wings.

"She's right, baby. When did you get so nosey?" His girl giggled as she gazed up at him, something he didn't notice because his eyes were too busy focused on me.

"I'm just saying. It's not a hard question, really."

"Vontae, what has gotten into you?" Aunt Hazel's tone held some censure in it, but not enough to actually make him listen.

"Nothing at all, ma. Just trying to catch up. Feels like I'm a little left behind."

"Must feel like seventh grade all over again then," I chuckled. Shorty almost choked. She wasn't the only one. Von's eyes held so much 'fuck you' energy, I was surprised he managed not to say it out loud. Everyone else within earshot at the table either looked shocked or was trying their best not to laugh. Considering my cousin hated being the butt of any joke, what I said only pissed him off more.

"Wanna run that by me again?"

Was the look he was giving me supposed to scare me? He should've known better. My original retort never came, getting lost when I felt a hand on my knee under the table.

Taking a peek next to me, I noticed Sinnamon subtly shaking her head. Fine.

"Just a joke, cuzzo. Relax."

In an attempt to lower the tension, it was my mama clearing her throat this time as she turned to Von's date. "So, Evie, how do you like the macaroni and cheese? I made it myself. Tried a little something different this year."

"Oh!" I guess she was caught off guard by anyone addressing her since my side of the table seemed to be everyone's focus. "It's really good. Probably some of the best I've ever had."

"You hear that, Hazel? *Some of the best she's ever had.*" My mother beamed with pride, and it made me smile. She always loved it when someone complimented her cooking. Loved it even more when someone did it in front of her sisters.

"I heard her. Doesn't mean one damn thing. She has nothing to compare it to."

"Fine." She shifted just enough to look next to me. "What do *you* think, Sin baby?"

We looked at each other. I thought about warning her, but clearly she was already well-versed at finding herself in the middle of the competition the sisters had going on.

"I have to admit, Aunt Vera. This might be some of the best mac and cheese you've ever brought to a family function." She took a bite and nodded. "Definitely the best." Quickly turning to Hazel, she added, "And mama, you put your foot in these greens! You know I'm gonna need a plate to take home, right?"

"Don't I always take care of you?" Hazel beamed, so

pleased with herself, she let the compliment thick mama had given to my mom go right through unchallenged.

It was so masterful I had to lean close, one arm slung over the back of her chair, to tell her just that.

"It's rude to whisper at a table full of people."

Goddamn. I'd never met a nigga as pressed as Von was right now.

"And y'all never answered my question."

Looking all types of exasperated, Sinnamon put down her fork and sat back. "And what question would that be, Vontae?"

"How exactly do y'all know each other?"

"Aww shit," Lennon whispered under his breath as he took a sip of his drink at the other end of the table. Sinnamon shot him a look.

"I didn't realize you two were familiar," Aunt Hazel said, confused.

"Really? Because they seemed awfully cozy when I walked in on them in the kitchen earlier." Von looked way too satisfied with himself, like he'd dropped some big secret.

"We actually just met, Auntie," I said, never breaking eye contact with her asshole of a son. "In fact, I have mama and Aunt Rose to thank for that."

"Me?" Rose asked.

"Yep. We crossed paths at the market when I went to go get the okra and whatnot y'all wanted. The line was so long, I didn't think I'd be able to get it, but she let me take advantage of her place in line and grab what I needed."

"Wait, this is the shorty whose shi— I mean stuff you bought the other day? The one you slid a few bills to?" Kal asked. He knew exactly what he was doing, adding that bit of information in there, but shit, I wasn't mad at all.

"The one and only," Sinnamon said with a smirk. "He was very…persuasive."

I chuckled at the throwback to our situation in the kitchen. That laugh was short-lived when Von decided to comment.

"Trickin' just to get some attention from a female. Damn, Gideon. Must be tough out here."

"Ain't nobody ever told you it ain't trickin' if you got it?" I shot back. "Damn, Vontae, guess you just don't have it or her, huh?"

"Okay, you two, that's enough," my father called from the other table. Everyone knew how Von and I could get once we started.

Even though I decided to chill, he made no such move. Everything I did or said required a smartass response, while everything Sinna said required his full attention. Shit, I started to feel bad for his actual date because he was paying her dust.

"Sinner, how about you tell Gideon here about the time we got locked in the attic last Christmas."

Everything about the look on her face told me she was irritated as fuck. "Ignore him." It didn't matter who was watching when I leaned over and pulled her chair closer to me to whisper the words into her ear.

Mumbling, she replied, "I wish it were that simple."

"What if I said I could help with that?"

She eyed me curiously, but I just winked and pulled back a little, my attention back on the toddler ass nigga across from us.

"You seem eager for me to know. Why don't you tell it?"

"Irritated?"

I wanted to knock the smug look off his fucking face, but what I had planned would give me and thick mama a lot more satisfaction.

"Not at all," I said, allowing one of my hands to slip under the table and find its way to Sinnamon's thigh. I felt it as her eyes took in my profile. Instead of returning the look, I caressed her bare skin, the way the sweater dress rose giving me perfect access. "From where I'm sitting, whatever happened in the past doesn't really hold much weight."

Silently willing her to open her legs a little wider with a firm grip and tug, my gaze stayed focused on my cousin, daring him to tell the story.

"Wait, last Christmas? Is that when you two were missing for like four hours?" Lennon asked, laughing into his glass.

"It wasn't funny, Lennon." Even though her words were directed toward the other end of the table, her thighs widened, giving me just enough room to slide between them. Fuck, her shit was warm. And here she was, playing along, daring me to finish what we'd started in the kitchen.

"Oh, come on, Sin. We had a good time, didn't we? I don't remember you complaining."

Von's words might've been meant to get a reaction from her, but it was my fingers sliding those panties to the side and moving against her clit that had her stifling a groan. I had to stop myself from smiling as she tried to cover the noise by taking a sip from her wine glass. That wasn't the best idea since the moment she did, my thumb stroked repeatedly against her clit, and she almost choked.

"Did y'all have a good time, Sinnamon?" I didn't give a fuck about her answer. I just needed an excuse to get a glimpse of her while I played with her beautiful pussy. Watching her squirm under my gaze had my dick hard as a brick again.

"I-I-I wouldn't call freezing my ass off up in the attic for four hours a g-good time." Her words came out in a hurry, like she was just saying the shit to get the focus off of her. Maybe that's exactly what she was doing because with every word, the glide and force of my thumb got more intense. I was going to make her come at this table if it was the last thing I did.

Von's eyes narrowed, suspicious, but before he could say anything, Aunt Hazel cut him off. "The only reason y'all were stuck up there so long was because you thought it would be cute to sit up there and do everything but grab the Christmas lights like I asked."

As soon as Von's eyes shifted away from her and everyone else at the table started throwing in their version of events, Sinna's hand dropped to grip mine. I could feel her thighs beginning to shake as my thumb slipped against the wetness I had her producing. I didn't know if she was trying to stop me or hold me in place, but it didn't matter.

"Now, Sinnamon." The shit might've been said in just a whisper, but I knew she could hear me. She shook her head, hell bent on fighting me, which only made me go harder.

Leaning in, not giving a fuck who might have been paying attention, I whispered, "I said *now*. Gimme that shit right here where everyone can see. Where Von can see."

My strokes became more insistent. If I could see it, I was sure it'd look like a blur with how fast I was going. The grip she had on my wrist tightened as she fought to keep her moan contained, a whimper sliding out of her as I felt her shit buck and gush as she came.

Both of us satisfied, she let go of my hand, trying to get her breathing back to normal. The look she gave me was a mix between 'What the fuck were you thinking?' and 'I'm about to fuck the shit out of you.' All I could do was smile as I brought my hand back up, using the other to readjust myself under the table. No one seemed to know what we'd just done. At least, that's what it seemed like since their conversation hadn't stopped. No one except Von. I knew he couldn't prove shit 'cause he didn't see anything, but he sure as fuck looked suspicious. I didn't give one shit, and I made sure both he and Sinnamon knew it when I brought my thumb to my lips and sucked her flavor clean off of it.

CHAPTER TWELVE

"WHAT THE FUCK ARE YOU DOING HERE WITH HIM, SIN?"

I knew Von was on some bullshit as soon as Sinna excused herself, probably to clean up after the mess I'd made of her, and he made up some reason to leave the table a couple minutes later. Kal shot me a look that said, "You finna handle that?" but of course, doing so was already on my radar.

After making my way upstairs, it didn't take long to find the spot where Vontae now called himself having her cornered. My jaw clenched at his tone 'cause who the fuck was he talking to? A smirk appeared on my face when my girl came out with the exact same thing.

"First of all, watch who you're talking to like that. You always seem to forget you don't run shit around here but your mouth."

"This is my mother's house."

"Exactly. Your mother's house, not yours. A home I was invited to and one I have every right to be in. Who I may or may not have shown up with is none of your business. I stopped being your business five months ago, remember?"

"Baby, you know you'll always be my business." Coming around the corner, it seemed like I was just in time to watch him reach out to caress her cheek as he backed her into the wall.

Her face told me shorty was truly disgusted. "Take your delusional ass on somewhere," she said, shoving him away from her. "You cheated on me, Vontae. Or did you forget?"

Fuck, I knew he didn't have the common sense his mama tried to give him, but he had to be completely out of it if what she was saying was true.

"Those other bitches didn't mean shit to me, Sin."

"So you keep saying, like I'm supposed to be flattered I'm the only *bitch* you had feelings for. That's not the flex you think it is, I promise you. Shit, for all I know, homegirl downstairs is one of the bitches who supposedly *didn't mean shit to you*."

"You know I wouldn't do that to you, baby."

She kissed her teeth. "I don't know a damn thing."

I watched as a switch flipped and he got in her face. "You really testing me, Sin. Like for real."

"See, maybe my memory ain't what the fuck it used to be." I chuckled as I made my presence known. "But correct me if I'm wrong. Didn't I say something earlier about watching your tone when you talk to her?"

Both of their eyes snapped to me. Though it was clear my lil' thick mama wasn't scared of Von, I still didn't like how my bitch ass cousin was pressing her.

"Moreover, I know for a fact you had the same lessons

about how to treat and talk to women that I did growing up. And yet, here you are, once again acting disrespectful."

"Didn't I tell you this ain't your fucking business, Gideon?" With his anger directed at me, he finally backed away from Sinna, changing course and heading my way.

"I guess we both hardheaded and don't listen 'cause I'm pretty sure I told you when it comes to Sinnamon, it's absolutely my business."

Flicking my eyes in her direction, I raised an eyebrow, silently asking her if she was good. She picked up on the message and gave me a nod.

"This little Captain Save-A-Hoe routine you're trying to put on is getting really tired."

Nothing about his act intimidated me. We both knew when it came down to it, I could and would rock his shit, no problem. It wouldn't be the first time, but out of respect for Aunt Hazel, I'd keep my hands to myself.

"Bruh, the only hoe I see around here is you. Fumbling thick mama and then begging her to take you back like a nineties R&B singer crying in the rain? Nigga, maybe you can't tell, but this ain't a music video. I promise you, she's good."

Two things happened at once. Sinnamon's eyes widened as she repeated my words on a whisper at the exact time Von's fist smashed into my face. There was a side of me that respected him for taking it there because despite all the mouth he had, never did I think he had it in him to actually throw hands. But my resolution to keep shit respectful in my aunt's house? I charged it. The last thing I would ever allow someone to do is put their hands on me. If he wanted to go blow for blow, I had no problem with that. From the look on his face, he knew exactly what the outcome was going to be.

My fist went flying into his jaw, the force behind it making him hit the wall and sending a couple of framed pictures crashing to the floor.

"Shit!" Sinnamon gasped, but I barely registered the sound as Von came flying at me again. This time my hit had him on the floor with the frames. As he struggled to get up, I made my way toward him, only to be stopped by a pair of arms gripping me from behind.

"Yo, chill!" Kal said, hold tightening.

"Nah, he wanna play big nigga on campus. Let's see if he's got what it takes."

"Man, fuck you and my sloppy ass seconds!" yelled Von as Lennon and my father pushed past me and helped him to his feet.

All his words did was set me off again as I yanked out of Kal's hold, seeing nothing but red. Set on giving him the actual ass whooping he deserved, I almost barreled straight into the very person he'd chosen to disrespect.

"Golds." I heard the words but still tried to move around her. "Golds!" This time when she yelled the name, she gripped my chin in her hand to ensure she had my full attention.

"Fuck. Him."

Her words seeped past the fog, but my eyes drifted behind her.

"Hey!" She yanked my chin, pulling my focus back to her, placing the softest kiss possible to my lips. "I said fuck him," she whispered against them before sucking my bottom lip into her mouth, kissing me like she didn't give a fuck about the audience around us. Maybe she didn't. Or maybe she knew the feel of her tongue slipping against mine was all the distraction I needed to forget about them. One hand found its way to her ass, palming the soft flesh, causing her to moan.

When she pulled away, making sure to give me one more peck, my eyes held her gaze. "You good?"

"I'm good," I answered and was surprised to find it was true.

"Are you fucking serious right now?" Remembering Von was still there, I looked up to see now he was the one being held back.

"Vontae! Watch your mouth." I couldn't be sure when it happened, but Aunt Hazel had made her way to the middle of the hallway, hands on her hips and warning in her tone.

"Me? I have to watch my fucking mouth while my girlfriend sits up here and hoes herself out to the next man?"

I'd never seen his mother move as fast as she did when she reached back and popped him in the mouth. "Don't you dare disrespect her or make me repeat myself. And last time I checked, Sinna was your *ex*-girlfriend, and you showed up here with another young lady on your arm." She nodded her head behind me, where Evie had apparently been standing on the stairs.

"Now, everyone is a bit heated...in more ways than one, it seems." That last bit was said while giving Sinna a look I couldn't quite decipher. I couldn't be sure if Aunt Hazel was trying to shame her, but the way shorty tucked herself into my side even more made her position clear: she didn't give a fuck what anyone had to say.

"Everybody go to their corners and just calm down,"

Aunt Hazel finished. "Let's just relax, collect ourselves, and enjoy the game with a bit of dessert."

It was looking like Von was going to test me and his mother in the same go, but instead, he shook off the hands gripping him and shouldered past me and down the stairs. A few seconds later, we heard the front door slam.

"I'll, umm... I'll go check on him." Evie turned, heading after him even though she honestly should've called a rideshare and took her ass home since he clearly didn't care.

Sinna pulled out of my grasp and made her way to Lennon while everyone else followed behind Evie, whispering in a way that let me know this was the only thing they were going to be talking about for the next couple of days.

"You sure you're good, bruh?" asked Kal.

Sneaking a glance at Lennon and Sinna, I nodded. "Yeah, I'm straight. Good look."

With a nod, he followed the rest of the group while I waited for Sinna to finish up her conversation.

"Behave," Lennon said, wiggling his eyebrows at me when he finally finished and walked by.

Once it was just the two of us in the hallway, Sinna closed the distance between us. As her fingers ghosted across my face, she worried her bottom lip.

"Come here. Let's get you cleaned up," she finally said, taking my hand in hers and leading me toward the door down the hall. We must have two definitions of what 'cleaned up' entailed as we entered the room and she flipped on the light. It wasn't a bathroom like I expected but a very familiar bedroom.

CHAPTER THIRTEEN

sinna

"YOU KNOW WHOSE ROOM THIS IS, RIGHT?"

I was very aware. In fact, after the little display in the hallway between Gideon and Von, I'd been hyperaware and very deliberate about what was behind this door and what I intended to do here.

Anytime Ms. Hazel managed to convince Von and I to stay overnight after one function or another, his old bedroom was always where we ended up. According to him, she hadn't changed a thing since he moved out on his own after college. Never wanted her baby boy to feel forgotten or replaced, I guess. Lucky for me, I didn't have the same hangup.

"I do." He made an attempt to walk toward me, but my hand shot out, stopping him in his tracks and pressing him back against the door.

"We need to head into the bathroom if you're going to get me cleaned up, ma."

"Okay," I said while pressing myself against him. That was absolutely on the agenda, but first...

This time, there was urgency in the kiss I gave him. Hunger had my body on fire, and I needed my fill of him before we made a move to do anything else. The shit I wanted to do to him, that I wanted done to me, did it have to be done in my ex's bedroom? Absolutely not. Was there something poetic about my desire to do so after watching this delicious man in front of me defend me the way he did? Hell fucking yes.

"You know I can take care of myself, right?" I asked on a gasp, pulling away.

"I know. I also know that ain't got shit to do with me 'cause you shouldn't have to. That nigga was gonna learn one way or the other." He leaned in, attempting to initiate another kiss, but I resisted.

"Learn what?"

"That we always gonna have a problem when he's fucking with what's mine."

My pussy clenched at his words. Any progress I'd made after leaving the table to get myself together after the orgasm he'd given me was ruined, just like the thin fabric covering my lower lips.

"I hope you're not expecting a thank you." Attitude was laced in my voice, but he chuckled, letting me know he didn't care.

"The fuck I look like? I did that shit because I wanted to, ma. Not to get some sort of reward out of it."

I hummed, finally allowing myself to lean back in. Instead of gracing him with a kiss, my tongue appeared and traced along his neck so I could taste him. The groan he let loose spoke to me, putting my whole body on notice.

"That's exactly why," I started, slipping a hand down the front of his pants, "you're going to get one." The minute I wrapped my hand around his girth, there wasn't a doubt in my mind. I was going to fuck this man right here, right now, in this room.

After his display at the dinner table, he was already ending the night with me riding him to kingdom come. Their little altercation just helped to speed up the timeline.

Dropping to my knees and taking his pants with me, my eyes never left his as I watched him lick his lips.

"You sure about this?"

"Very." His briefs were next, and I swear my mouth watered when his thick black dick came into view.

"And if I asked who's this for?"

It wasn't hard to figure out what he was really asking. Was I about to suck his dick to piss off Vontae even further or to please the man in front of me? Truthfully, it was both. Hearing the way he talked about me, the way he checked his cousin over me had me wanting to do something reckless. What fit the bill better than this? At the same time, everything about this man pulled me in and mesmerized me. I wanted him regardless of the time, place, or situation. The fact that it was a silent fuck you to his cousin was an added bonus. It was the best of both worlds. We had to be quick, though. There was only so long we could be away from the group before someone started to wonder where we were. They were probably already trying to figure it out.

"I'd say, does it really matter?" Swiping my thumb across the tip of his dick to collect the precum that had begun to pool there, I used it to ease the friction as I began to stroke him. "Because I'm going to give you this pussy regardless. Might as well start here."

To prove my point, I flicked my tongue across his tip

while dipping my free hand beneath my own panties and swiping at my clit. "And I'm dripping for you, just like you're dripping for me, Golds. So are you really about to tell me no?"

His lids lowered with need. "Shit, say less, ma, and get to work then."

He didn't have to tell me twice.

Gathering every bit of saliva I had, I let it drip down along his shaft before immediately slipping him into my mouth. His stifled groan as I suckled lightly on his tip was music to my ears. I wanted his shit soaked, taking my time lapping at every inch of him with my tongue before taking him back into my mouth and letting his dick slide down my throat.

"That's right, suck my shit." His words came out as groans, egging me on as I bobbed up and down on his length. Every time he slid along my tongue, it sent shock-waves through my pussy.

Without making the conscious choice to do so, I pulled him from my mouth. Taking my hand from between my legs, I transferred the juices coating my fingers onto his dick.

"Your freaky ass," he chuckled as I swallowed his dick once again. The way he tasted, his salty glaze mixed with mine, had me moaning uncontrollably. We tasted so fucking good, but I wanted more.

"Come for me," I begged, massaging his balls with my hand. He cursed at the feel of me suckling his tip again. "I wanna taste it."

"Nah." He snatched me up with so much force my head was swimming. "You can swallow my shit later. After I feel you wrapped around me."

My back slammed into the door as he ripped my panties clean off. A whimper escaped my lips as he lifted me up, hands under my thighs, gripping me tight. "Put it in."

This man loved to give directions, and so help me, I wanted to follow every one of them. Reaching between us, I gripped his hard, wet length and tapped it against my clit.

"Oooh shit."

"I swear I'm about to tear your shit up. Keep playing with me," he said through gritted teeth.

"Promises, *promisessss*." The last word ended on a hiss as he slipped into my entrance.

"Goddamn," Gideon groaned, his forehead falling forward against my neck.

I was at a loss for words. Having him down my throat was one thing. This though? This feeling had me wanting to scream the house down. The slight burn from how he was stretching me hurt in the best possible way. Every single nerve ending I had seemed two seconds away from being set off.

"*Fuck.* I need a minute." He braced his hand against the door, and I whined in protest.

"I want it now." My legs locked around him, making him sink even deeper. Whining my hips in a steady motion, I taunted him. "I thought you wanted to fuck me, Golds. Don't you wanna fuck me?"

His growl was answer enough. "You keep that up and this won't last much longer," he admitted. "It's been a minute, and I swear this shit is too fucking wet."

Shooting him a wicked grin, only one response came to mind. "Guess you better make it worth my while, then."

No more motivation necessary, he pulled himself out

just enough to thrust back into me. "Again," I gasped, but he was already answering my request with another forceful stroke. Letting my head fall back against the door, I tried to catch my breath.

"He fucked up when he let you go, didn't he, ma?" His breath fanned against my pulse point. I didn't expect the sharp sting of his teeth sinking into my skin, and I cried out before I could clamp my mouth shut.

"Didn't he?" Gideon asked again.

The door had to be rattling for the punishing pace he was setting.

"Uh-huh," I nodded in agreement. My eyelids fluttered closed as my eyes rolled into the back of my head.

"And you fucked up when you let me in this mother-fucka, didn't you?"

"I *diiiiid.*" A moan slipped from my lips. "Fuck, Golds."

His hands clamped down on my hips as he bounced me up and down his dick. I held on for dear life, hands buried deep in his locs. What was it he said about this not lasting? Fuck, maybe that was a good thing. Too much more of this and I'd be climbing the goddamn walls.

It was taking every bit of restraint I had not to moan out loud. Even my whimpers sounded like screams to my own ears. I pitched myself forward, letting my head fall into the crook of his neck.

"You was just talking all that shit, Sinnamon. Now you gotta back it up. Wet my shit up 'cause I promise you I'm finna paint your fucking walls."

He buried himself to the hilt, leaving it to me to use him as I saw fit. Grinding against him at just the right angle had his thick length tapping against my g-spot while his pelvis gave me the perfect amount of friction against my clit.

The combination sent me right off the cliff, and the only way I could stifle my moans was by biting into his neck. He hissed and used his grip on my thighs to lift me up as his dick slipped out and he came against my inner thigh.

After using my tongue to soothe the spot where I'd bitten him, I pulled away. Before I could say a word, I was pressed right back up against the door with Gideon's hand wrapped around my neck as he devoured me with a kiss. The way he sucked on my tongue and let me glide it over his grill made me want to say fuck it and go for another round.

"This my shit now," he said, breaking the kiss.

I was out of breath but still managed to retort, "Is that what you think?"

"Shorty, that's what I *know*."

CHAPTER FOURTEEN

sinna

"Bitch, you nasty as hell."

Maybe I should have been offended those were the first words out of Lennon's mouth when I finally found my way back downstairs and out onto the patio with him. Then again, considering I just let one of his cousins dick me down *raw* in his other cousin's childhood bedroom...nasty was probably putting it mildly.

"Fuck you," I laughed, and he screwed up his face.

"You didn't get enough of that from Gideon? Oh, my bad, *Golds*."

I couldn't even muster up an attitude or shame. "Do you think anyone else noticed?"

"I think a few invested parties could make an educated guess." He turned to look into the house. "And one of those parties absolutely did after he stormed into the house looking for you and stormed right back out once he realized both of y'all were missing."

The petty part of me was happy to hear it. Let him wonder where we were and what we were doing. I meant it when I said I wasn't his business anymore, and maybe now, he'd know I meant it.

"I can see you're absolutely elated at the prospect. You'll be even happier to know when he came back, it was alone, so I'm pretty sure his date left him right there on the curb."

Elated wasn't exactly the right word, mostly because whether I knew her or not, no part of me believed Evie deserved to have to watch her boyfriend fight over another woman.

"But I do think you might want to talk to one other person before you leave for the night." He eyed me suspiciously. "That was me assuming you came out here to let me know you're leaving so you can go do more unmentionable things with my cousin somewhere other than my auntie's house."

"Next time I see you, remind me to give you a gold star for being so smart."

"No gold star necessary. I'll take pie as payment."

Rolling my eyes, I asked, "Where is she?" No explanation was needed on who "she" was.

"Well, *she* let everyone loose on the dessert table right about the time Von realized you and Gideon were still missing, so if I had to guess, probably on the front porch trying to eat her pie in peace."

After promising to call him and set a date to hang out for happy hour, I went back into the house.

"Meet you at your place after I drop Kal off?"

Just the promise of what was to come based on Gideon's question had me ready to jump him. My lack of underwear, though, made me ramp those hormones down as best I could.

"Mmmm, yes, please. There's one thing I need to take care of first, though."

"I got you." For a split second, the thought of not kissing him crossed my mind, but at this point, we didn't really have shit to hide.

After giving Gideon a quick kiss, I cut a path through the house that would take me to the front. Just as Lennon promised, Mama Hazel was seated on the porch, a plate with a big ass slice of pie perched happily in her hand.

"On a scale of one to ten, how bad am I in trouble right now?"

Her laugh broke the silence that followed. "For which activity? Having a hand in starting a fight between my son and my nephew? Or sneaking away with said nephew to do God knows what?" My mouth opened to say something, but she stopped me, hand raised. "That was not an invitation to tell me what you did or didn't do, baby. I was your age once, I did my share of slick shit."

Snapping my lips shut, I took a seat as she patted the space next to her. "Maybe you should be in trouble for putting your whole ass ankle in this pie *yet again* because now I'm gonna have to fight my sisters so neither one of them can take one out of here."

Now it was my turn to laugh. Leaning my head against her shoulder, I snuggled close. "I'm sorry your holiday turned into such a mess, mama. And for my role in the mess."

Sitting her plate down, she placed her head on top of mine. "I think we've already established that I'm the one who was leading the mess today. You don't have anything to apologize for. You're grown, and so is Gideon." She sighed. "And despite the way he tends to act, so is my son.

If he can't see what a prize you are but that boy in there can, well…who am I to judge?"

This was why I loved her. Did she meddle where she had no business? Yes. But at least she could own up to it and the fact she was wrong.

"But next time, at least wait 'til y'all get home before you let him bend you five ways from Sunday. I thought I was done having to deal with that once you and Vontae ended."

"Mama!" I shrieked.

"Don't *mama* me! All that bumping you were doing against the door, it's not like it was a secret."

Groaning, I hid my face in her shoulder. "I'll keep that in mind."

"Good. Now, leave me be, little girl. I'd like to enjoy my pie before I have to call and curse my son out for his behavior."

Standing with a laugh, I gave her a quick kiss on the cheek. "Happy Thanksgiving, mama."

"Happy Thanksgiving, baby."

CHAPTER FIFTEEN

gideon

"WE'RE ABOUT TO HEAD OUT, MA." WALKING INTO THE family room with Kal, I found my mother sitting in my father's lap cackling about something, probably at my Aunt Rose's expense since she was sitting next to my uncle pouting.

"We as in you and Kal or you and Sinna?" she asked slyly.

"Kal." Considering he was the one standing next to me, she should've known the answer to that question.

"Well, don't say it like that! Shoot, all the noise the two of y'all had going on upstairs, I just had to ask." This time when she cackled, she wasn't alone.

"Ma, please chill," I said, shaking my head.

My pops swatted at her, the only one who didn't seem to find what she said funny. "Vera, leave the boy alone." Before I could thank him for having my back, he added, "Now that he's solidified he's the better man on Von's turf, he's just going to meet her at her place." And of course they couldn't help but laugh. Even Kal chuckled, earning him a look of his own.

This nigga. "Really, pops? You finna do me like that?"

"Did I lie?"

When I didn't answer because okay, yeah, he had a point, he chuckled. "Exactly. I'm not knocking it, just keeping it real."

"Whatever. That's what I get for coming over here to say bye to y'all."

"Awww, come here, baby. You know we're just playing." My mother stood, and despite her jokes, I didn't resist when she reached in for a hug. "I like Sinna. Always have. Now, I can't say all this drama between the two of you and Von is my cup of tea." The snort that left me was out of my control. We all knew how much my mother loved drama. "But Sinna has always been a sweetheart and way too good for Von anyway." She smirked at me, a mischievous twinkle in her eyes. "And now I'm the one that gets to brag about how my daughter-in-law is the master of sweet potato pies."

"Daughter-in-law? Ma, we haven't even gone on a date yet. Don't you think you're getting a little ahead of yourself?"

"Between the ruckus y'all were making and the way you knocked that lil' boy on his ass, it seems to me she's right on track," Aunt Rose chimed in.

That was officially my cue to get the hell up out of there and I made sure they knew it. After letting my parents know not to expect either Kal or I back at the house since he said he had a shorty of his own to meet up with, we grabbed a few to-go plates, then headed out to the car.

"You know it's absolutely wild you took your cousin's girl *and* knocked her down in his mom's house, right? After beating his ass at that," chuckled Kal as we made our way to his destination.

"First, she's not his girl anymore. That shit was dead long before I came around. Second, you know it didn't even go down like that. I didn't even know who she was when we met."

"Yeah, but you weren't going to let that shit stop you once you found out."

"Damn right, I wasn't. Just 'cause he fumbled Sinnamon doesn't mean I'm about to."

"And fucking her in his mother's house?"

"Was not planned!" I laughed. "But again, I was not about to let the fact we were in his old room stop me once she made it known what type of time she was on." Shorty was on demon time and got her lick back in spades. I was not mad at all.

"His room, nigga? Yeah, you on some wild boy shit, Gids."

There was nothing to do except chuckle and shrug. He wasn't lying, but I was just following thick mama's lead and would absolutely do it again.

After dropping him off where he needed to go and putting in the address Sinnamon sent, I made my way to her apartment. What I saw once she buzzed me up and I made it to her front door only made me double down on what I already knew: I wouldn't change one mother-fucking thing about today.

It should have been a crime the way she looked, arm raised above her head as she used it to lean against the door, a short burnt orange silk robe untied and open to showcase a matching lace bra and panty set. She had every curve and dimple on display, not an ounce of shyness to her because she knew, just like I did, that she looked beyond fucking beautiful. A groan left me as I felt my shit go rock hard.

"Is this how you greet all your guests, Sinnamon?"

"Only the ones who love to talk shit and wear golds. There may have been a few of those." Her smirk might have been teasing but shit, I didn't really give a fuck who'd seen this view before me. I was the one seeing it now and for the foreseeable future. Any other shit wasn't of consequence to me.

"Well, get your fine ass back in the house before one of them niggas show up and I gotta handle they asses."

Giggling, she backed away to let me through the threshold. Not wanting her to get too far, I reached out and grabbed her lightly by the neck.

"Gimme a kiss," I said, closing the door behind me.

"That's how you talk to strangers?" she quipped, taking it back to what she'd said to me just a few days ago.

"Nah." I used my grip to pull her in close and pressed my lips firmly against hers. She tasted just like her new namesake, the spice dancing on my tongue as it tangled with hers. "Just how I talk to my thick mama," I finished once I finally pulled away to let her catch her breath.

"Mmmm, and what else do you want to do to your thick mama?" Her tongue snaked across her lips like she was still hungry for whatever flavor I'd left behind.

"I have a few ideas. Bending you over so I can tear that ass up from the back is at the top of the list." The same glint she'd had earlier in the day appeared again. "But first, I know you've got a slice of pie waiting for me, right?"

"Boy!" Calling herself snatching away from me, Sinna cocked her head sideways. "I'm standing in front of you looking like a certified appetizer, entrée, and snack," she said incredulously, "and you wanna talk to me about pie?"

"What can I say? I like to have my dessert first."

Kissing her teeth, she turned to leave. "I should put your black ass out, playing with me like this."

Snickering, I followed behind her, my eyes immediately going to the way her ass peeked out from the bottom of her robe. I couldn't imagine a scenario where a nigga could get tired of looking at or gripping her. Each cheek was more than a handful, and as soft and luscious as it was, keeping my hands off of it was not an option. To prove my point, I pulled up behind her, hard dick pressed firmly against her ass while my hand slid down to cop a feel.

"How you mad at me because I'm giving in to all the hype over your pie, Sinnamon? Not to mention, I could taste that shit on your tongue, so I know you've been in here dipping in it yourself. You not trying to share with me?"

Instead of answering, she just shot me an irritated look over her shoulder, though we both knew there was no real heat behind it.

"Would it help my case if I said I wanna know what you taste like when I still have the flavor of your second-best dessert on my tongue? Because I know it's about to be delicious as fuck."

"Second best? What's the first?"

"Your pussy of course."

Twisting herself around and out of my reach as we hit her kitchen, she thought about it for a second. "You are so full of it." Sinna made her way over to one of the counters and took the top off of a dessert stand. "But I'll let you have a slice anyway. Just know you're absolutely going to have to make good on that promise to taste me on your tongue."

"Bet." I reached into my pocket and pulled out one of the blunts Kal rolled that morning. "You trying to hit this?"

"Now see, you should've just started with that." Laughing, she pointed me in the direction of her balcony and let me know she'd meet me out there once she cut us a couple of slices.

The temperature had dipped, and while I was comfortable thanks to my sweatshirt and jacket, I didn't want shorty coming out here and freezing her pretty ass off.

"Aye, thick mama, make sure you bring a blanket out here to stay warm," I called over my shoulder as I made my move to light the blunt.

"Shouldn't it be your job to keep me warm?" Her voice caught me off guard, but the sight of her was enough to set me at ease.

"Oh, trust, I can absolutely handle that."

CHAPTER SIXTEEN

"I LOVE HOW FUCKING RIGHT I WAS."

After meeting me on the balcony, my lil' baby planted herself in the chair next to me, wrapped in a blanket just like I'd suggested. With her legs stretched out across my lap, smoke billowing from her lips, she looked relaxed and in her element.

"Right about what?"

"That you were the type of nigga to talk big shit with a big dick to match," she answered.

The boom of laughter I released had to have been heard by her neighbors. "Yo, you got all of that from one little comment?"

"Nigga, you just said, and I quote, 'this pie is aight, but fighting over it is wild.' Matter of fact, give me back my plate and get out since my shit is just *aight*."

She stood, dropping the blanket on her chair, and took the step and a half it took to get to me. Before she could snatch the half-empty plate from my hand, I grabbed her, bringing her down so she was straddling my lap.

"You know I'm just playing, thick mama." Taking the blunt from her, I took my own pull before putting it out in the tray. We both had a nice buzz going, and I was sure my eyes were just as low as hers.

"I don't know shit." The way she had her lip poked out was cute as fuck. All the pouting she was doing was nothing but a turn-on.

"Put that lip back in before I give you something to pout about for real." My hand smacked against her thigh.

"Boy, you ain't finna do a damn thing."

Raising an eyebrow, I chuckled. "Yeah, aight. Keep thinking that."

We sat for a while, letting the silence grow between us for a few minutes before I decided to free up my other hand and set the plate down on the small table next to us. Now that they were both empty, my hands moved up and gripped her ass, kneading and massaging each cheek as I watched Sinna's eyes gradually close and her hands came to rest against my chest.

"It's probably a little late for me to say this, but I need you to know today wasn't about my fuck ass cousin for me. And it wasn't just me tryna run game on you to get my shit wet, either."

When she didn't respond right away, I thought she might not believe me.

"That's what you think today was about for me?" Her eyes opened and stared down at me.

It had crossed my mind. Fucking me once she knew who I was would have been the ultimate lick. Remembering what she'd said at Aunt Hazel's house though, I shook my head. "Nah, not completely. Even if it was, though, it wouldn't bother me because in the end, it got me what I wanted anyway."

"And what, pray tell, would that be?"

"A chance to get to know you." The look she gave me said she didn't believe that shit, making me laugh. "I'm serious, Sinna. Don't get me wrong, the pussy is phenomenal." She giggled. "But I also like your vibe. After I fucked around at the market, I told myself if the opportunity to get at you ever came up again, I was taking it. Your energy, the way you carry yourself, all of that shit keeps drawing me in."

"Okay, but you don't even live here, Gideon. This day has been a lot more fun than I expected it to be and your whole energy is a vibe as well, but realistically, what's the timeline on this? Because if you're just saying shit you think I want to hear, it's unnecessary. I'm not expecting you to make this anything beyond what it is tonight."

"And I appreciate that, but respectfully, I'm grown. So if I say I'm trying to get to know you, then I mean it. I don't give a fuck where I live or who you used to fuck with." She leaned in, allowing me to place a quick kiss on her lips. "Just ride this wave with me."

Smirking, she said, "Okay, then. We can do that, but, uh…right now, I'm tryna ride something else too."

"Shit, you ain't said nothing but a word." Laying a firm smack against her ass, I added, "Get your ass back inside so you can sit that pretty pussy on my face."

The instruction only needed to be given once. Within minutes of us going back into the apartment, I was laying on the couch face up as she ground her hips and drenched me from above. The sounds of my lips smacking mixed with her curses and whimpers filled the apartment. It made me hard as fuck knowing she had every bit of her weight on top of me, trusting I could handle it. It didn't seem like the thought of squatting or hovering even occurred to her. She knew when I said 'sit on my face,' that was exactly what I meant.

My tongue slipped between her folds, alternating between dipping inside of her and caressing her clit. I needed to taste her cum more than I needed air. The shit was essential to my survival, made clear by the way my arms locked around her thighs, holding her in place as she started to try and shift out of my grasp.

"Umph, baby, *please*." The sounds falling from her lips were muffled thanks to her thighs squeezing tight over both ears, but I could hear her just enough to understand. Every whine and whimper just pushed me to go harder.

"This shit is too fucking good. *Ooooh fuck*!"

She may have been the one to say it out loud, but the way each drop of her flavor settled against my tongue had me thinking the same damn thing. I was determined to pull that nut from her. It was the only thing on my mind.

As her fingers buried themselves in my locs, I groaned and opened my eyes, catching the exact moment she gazed down, watching me devour her. The look on her face began to change, brow furrowing in concentration as she stopped fighting me and instead gave over to the feeling.

"I'm co—" She gasped, seemingly out of breath. "*Shit, Golds. Fu*—"

If her words didn't prepare me for the way she flooded my tongue, the tremors in her thighs damn sure would have.

Once I had my fill, my grip loosened, lips kissing

along her inner thigh as my tongue darted out every few seconds to clean up the mess we'd made there.

"You might have been right about me," I said as she slipped down until our bodies were aligned. "But I was right, too."

"About what?" She peppered kisses all around my face, paying special attention to my lips and sucking my tongue, savoring the taste of herself there.

"About the fact that the combination of your pie and my Sinnamon is delicious as fuck."

Laughter burst from her chest, and the shit was contagious because my smirk turned into a full-bodied laugh immediately.

"You are so goddamn annoying."

"Call me anything you want as long as you put Golds behind it, shorty."

"Fine. You are so goddamn annoying, *Golds*." Her words might have been saying one thing, but I knew she didn't mean the shit for real.

"Let's see how annoying I am when you're ending Thanksgiving with my dick buried deep inside of you."

"Sounds like the perfect end to a wild ass day if you ask me." Her hands reached into my pants, a grunt leaving me as soon as her fingers wrapped around my shaft.

I was beginning to understand why Thanksgiving was Vontae's favorite holiday. It had quickly become mine, too.

*want more of your
favorite messy duo?*

You're in luck. Turns out hooking up with your ex-boyfriend's cousin at Thanksgiving isn't just the ultimate lick back. It's also the perfect way to fall in love.

Grab my holiday short, Szn's Greetings, and catch up with Sinna and Gideon as they celebrate Christmas a year after their Thanksgiving shenanigans.

a final word

THANK YOU FOR READING SINNAMON & GOLDS. THIS WAS my first attempt at a holiday novella and thanks to Kai and Tanon, I got to make it a messy one. This was so much fun and I hope you laughed and got just as much satisfaction out of this as I did.

If you're able, please find the time to leave a rating and/or review on your favorite platform (Amazon, Goodreads, Storygraph, etc.). They're the best way to help readers find new favorites and so important when supporting indie authors.

To keep up-to-date on upcoming Lady Marie projects, be sure to sign up for the Spice In Your Life Newsletter, check out my linktree, and follow me on social media @ladymariewrites.

. . .

To order a signed copy of any of my paperback projects, merch, or web exclusives, please visit the Lady Marie Shop at ladymariewrites.com

acknowledgments

At this point what I'm about to say shouldn't even be a surprise anymore. Thank you to Kai, Sissa, Tanon, and Shon for always being in my writing corner with every project. Y'all keep me writing even when I'm not sure I can.

Also, a special thank you to my ARC readers Jaleesa, Lee, Mychelé, Taima, Ciera, and Mel. Your energy for this project and willingness to lay your eyes on it before anyone else is greatly appreciated. The way you support Black indie authors is unmatched!

And finally, thank you to the readers because without you, no project would ever be possible.

also by lady marie

SISTERS & SERENDIPITY SERIES

Worth It (A Fake Dating Novel)

Found Forever (An Established Couple, After the HEA Novella)

SUGARED AND SPICED SERIES

Sugar, Sugar (An Age Gap, Sugar Arrangement Novella)

Sweet Heat (A FFM Age Gap, Sugar Arrangement Novella)

Sugar-Coated Kisses (An Age Gap Insta-love Novella)

Sweet Control (An Age Gap, Sugar Arrangement Novella)

SLEIGH THE NIGHT COLLECTION

After Tonight (A Brother's Best Friend Novella, *Sleigh the Night* Prequel)

Sleigh the Night (A Winter Shorts Collection)

HOLIDAY NOVELLAS AND SHORT STORIES

With Sugar on Top (A Sugared and Spiced NYE Short)

Sinnamon & Golds (A Lick Back Season, Thanksgiving Novella)

Szn's Greetings (A Sinnamon & Golds Christmas Short)

Resolutions (A New Year's Novellette)